Raven

Terrence Brejla

Channing Way Press/San Francisco

Terrence Brejla

Raven

This book is with love for Melissa, My Chapter Two

Terrence Brejla

Life is good.
Death is peaceful.
It's the transition that's troublesome.
                    Isaac Asimov

Hell is a place where nothing connects with nothing.
          T.S. Eliot. Introduction to Dante's *Inferno*

One

It was one of those clear, bright summer mornings we get in California in the early spring before the high fog sets in. The rains are finally over. The hills are still green and the valleys lush. The tourists are starting to return to San Francisco. I had recently moved my office into a small walk-up on Bridgeway in Sausalito. It's the first town you come to when you cross the Golden Gate Bridge north into Marin County, and it looks like an Italian fishing village.

My name is Scott Butler, and I'm an attorney. When I tell people what I do for a living I get an even split of groans and admiration. I fought hard to make it through Law School at Cal. I could have opted for an easier school, but got admitted to Cal and decided to go for the brass ring. It was a tough fight, but I got through. My grades weren't at the top of my class, but I passed the California Bar on my first attempt which was more than a lot of my classmates could boast. I'm a good lawyer and a zealous advocate for my clients. I still enjoy practicing the law. Many of my friends from law school have given up on law and are doing something else. I could never consider doing something like that, at least not quite yet.

Life is good. I had the good sense to marry my college sweetheart, Julie. She never fails to remind me that she's too good for me. I agree and have no idea why she ever agreed to marry a guy like me. Julie has a killer body and a luscious head of black curly hair. Now in her early 40s, she's still a head turner. I just turned 46 and am having a difficult time staring at 50 coming quickly around the corner. I'm 5'11" and pride myself for being in good shape. My dog, Emma, an Australian Cattle Dog, enjoys long walks along the water. I need to indulge her more often. Other than Julie she's the only female who has ever completely understood me. That includes my Mom, who was always very patient, but to this date still shakes her head when she tries to comprehend what I have chosen as my life's work.

Julie is a fourth generation San Franciscan. She's the kind of person everyone instantly likes when they meet her. She has everything going for her. She's beautiful, spot-on smart, and is a very nice person. She was largely raised by her paternal grandmother who taught her in her teens how to ski and play golf. She was a bigger than life figure who had a profound influence on who Julie is today.

After graduation from St. Ignatius College Prep she enrolled at Cal. All she ever wanted to be was a teacher and majored in education. She is one of those rare people that were able to get through Cal in three and a half years with a 4.0 average no less. She rowed crew for her entire time at Cal. She enjoyed the exhilaration of getting up at the crack of dawn and being with her friends on the water. She was also active in her sorority, Kappa Kappa Gamma. How she found time to keep everything under control I will never know.

After Cal Julie and I didn't see each other for a couple of years. We had a falling out and she decided to go out and try to save the world. She joined the Peace Corps and apparently went to a small country in the Middle East, Bahrain. We were largely out of contact for those years except for an occasional Christmas or birthday card. I thought it odd that she made no effort to stay in touch nor chose to tell me a lot about what she had done upon her return even to this day. I wondered what she might have been hiding. When she returned we reunited and picked up where we left off and were engaged six months later. We had a lavish San Francisco wedding and went to Maui on our honeymoon.

Julie and I moved to Sausalito about ten years ago from the Mission District in San Francisco. We bought an old Victorian built in 1867. It had been built as a Methodist church and converted to a residence in the 1920s. It has a great view of the Bay and sits on a long skinny lot with a charming red barn at the back. The house was landlocked, and unfortunately we have to park on the street behind the property and walk down a steep hill that is actually a private road. This is the only thing that was wrong with an almost perfect house. Once down the hill, I have to walk through my neighbor, Nancy Drew's carport to get to my house. Yes, that is really her name.

We made a lot of good decisions and a few that we regretted, one being not having children. It's not that we ever made a conscious decision to not have children; it just never happened. I thought Julie blamed me for this sadness, but she never came out and said so. I always thought I was too busy for kids. Actually I was afraid that I wouldn't be a good father. Unfortunately I didn't have a good role model. Although my father and I became closer in the past few years, he had been a distant presence in my life for as long as I could remember. We had to work hard to get the relationship we have today. My father is actually a good guy and now realizes what he lost by never being around. He put the almighty dollar ahead of his family. Julie kept thinking we had one final shot at having a family. I wasn't so sure.

Julie had been a school teacher, having spent nine years teaching second grade at St. Hillary's Catholic School in neighboring Tiburon. A couple years ago she confessed that she had burned out on teaching and wanted to try her hand at her own business. She was a gifted teacher. The kids and their parents loved her, but it was time to move on. They tried to talk her into staying but her mind was made up.

Her passion is needlepoint, and I helped her open a needlepoint shop on Caledonia Street, about two blocks from home. She decorated it herself and did a great job. She modeled it after a small shop we had visited in the Kensington District of London. Julie worked in the shop Monday through Thursday and had a couple of friends cover for her Friday through Sunday. "Julie's Needlepoint Shop" took off very quickly. It surpassed our sales goals each month. Julie has a keen mind, and I never had any doubt about her ability to pull this off. We didn't go into this with the thought of getting rich, but the extra money certainly has helped. Everyone seems to think that every attorney is rolling in dough. That's not always the case. I have a couple things I do from time to time to get some extra money. These are things I'm not proud of, but you've got to do what you've got to do.

My primary practice is litigation. I'm the guy someone comes to when they want to sue someone, and I have the reputation of being very aggressive. That's true. I typically prevail when a case goes to trial, but I prefer to negotiate. I've done a good job of networking is Sausalito. I sit on a couple commissions and am a close friend of most city council members. As a result I am hired frequently by the city when they need some extra fire power, which as of late has been quite often.

I am currently representing the city in a suit against the owner of the old Alta Mira Hotel who has converted the property into an exclusive drug and alcohol rehab center. The residents are up in arms and are trying to close the place down. This is going to be a hard one to win. The owner has done nothing illegal. The State of California licensed the property to operate. I'm not sure how I'm going to fight this battle. I'll think of something. I hate to lose. My friends and neighbors in Sausalito seem to always be upset about one thing or another. When this problem came to a boil they called a special town meeting where almost one thousand people showed up. That's a thousand people out of a town with a population of only seventy-five hundred. The good people of Sausalito always enjoy getting together en masse to complain about something they deem outrageous.

It was late in the day, about 4.PM. A member of the City Council stopped by about an hour ago to talk about the case dealing with the Alta Mira. His name is Howie Steiner, and he loves to talk and talk and talk. In about 15 minutes we covered everything we had to talk about, but he just wanted to chat. He was the client so I had to be polite and indulge him. I didn't bill the City for the whole time he was there. I entered a half hour on my time sheet. Howie was a pleasant old guy, and I didn't mind giving him an opportunity to speak his mind. He invited me to go fishing with him the following week. Although I had no intention of doing so, I told him I would think about it.

About 20 minutes after Howie walked down the steps the phone rang. It was Julie. "So what are you doing, mister?" she asked.

"I'm just sitting here sitting here thinking of you." I responded.

"Oh, you are such a sweet talker. Why don't we meet at Paradise Bay for dinner?" It was a restaurant we liked near our house. My friend Charlie Henderson opened it about five years ago. It had a deck with a great view outback. Unfortunately it was a little too cool today to sit outside.

"What time?" I asked.

"How about 5:30? I'll close the shop early. I've had two customers all day."

"Any sales? Sounds like it wasn't worth opening."

"Unfortunately when you're in retail you've got to open every day no matter what. It gives me time to catch up on my reading. My friend Megan came in and bought about ten dollars worth of needlepoint that I had marked down. It was some really ugly stuff that I was glad to get rid of. I'm not sure why I bought it in the first place"

"See you soon."

I checked my email and answered three new ones that were waiting. I was glad there were only three. One was from my brother Ted in Chicago, another from a prospective client, and a third from an investigator who was working with me on the Alta Mira case. He wanted to meet that evening. I was too tired and begged off until tomorrow morning. Besides I was on my way to meet Julie and didn't want to disappoint her. Lately we didn't spend as much time together as I would like. We had been talking some time about taking a vacation but I was never able to carve out the time.

I typically walk to the office each day. It was about five blocks from home to the office. That was one of the cool things about living in a place like Sausalito. I locked the door and headed down the stairs to Bridgeway and headed north towards Paradise Bay. It was a chamber of commerce type day. The weather was almost perfect. The shops were full. The ferry from San Francisco was arriving across the street. A combination of tourists and Sausalito residents who worked in The City poured off the ferry. Another day was winding down in Sausalito. Little did I know that mine still had a long way to go.

It happened right before I arrived at Paradise Bay. I had a sharp shooting pain on the right side of my abdomen. It was similar to the pain I experienced when I had a kidney stone last year, only a lot worse. Unlike the kidney stone it came and went and then came and disappeared once more. I sat down on a bus bench, caught my breath, and then entered the restaurant and found Julie sitting at a table by the window. She got up as I approached the table and gave me a hug.

"What's wrong, Scott? You look terrible."

"You sure know how to make a guy feel good,"

"Are you okay?"

"I think so."

I explained what had happened just moments ago.

"Think I should drive you to the ER?"

"No. Of course not. This will pass. I'll be okay." In reality I wasn't so sure.

Our waiter approached the table. He was a young Hispanic man with a toothy smile. We ordered cocktails. The pain was still there but tolerable. Against my better judgment I had two drinks which did little to dull the pain. Waiting for our food we engaged in some meaningless conversation. Then the pain hit me again, this time a lot harder. Julie saw the painful look on my face. It was obviously something more serious than I had thought she was concerned.

"Sit right there," she said. "I'm going home to get the car. We're going to the ER."

I muttered a feeble protest but knew she was right. She returned minutes later. She briefly stopped and told Charlie she was taking me to the hospital and that she'd stop by later to pay the Check. Charlie said to not worry about it. He'd pick up the Check.

Julie brought my black Jaguar. It would have been too tight given my condition to squeeze into her Chrysler Crossfire. We headed over the Golden Gate Bridge towards UCSF, the University of California San Francisco Medical Center. Julie zipped through the FasTrak toll plaza turned right on 19th Street and then a turn on Clement and looped around on Geary towards the hospital. The pain was getting worse. I wondered how long it would be before they could see me. She pulled into the parking by the ER.

"Can you make it in by yourself?" she asked. "Shall I get a wheel chair?"

"I think I can make it." I actually had my doubts. I shuffled slowly towards the door. Every step hurt more than the last one. I stopped a couple times to catch my breath.

We made it to the automatic door and entered. Julie walked to the receptionist and told her I was in terrible pain. The receptionist took some basic information and led us to another clerk who pulled up insurance information from our UCSF profile. A nurse came and led me to an exam room. I was thrilled they didn't make us go back out to the waiting room. I was anxious to get some meds that would dull the pain. There were other patients who were there before we arrived who weren't too happy that we were given preferential treatment.

Moments later a young man in green scrubs walked in. and said his name was Dr. Toby Pratt, and that he was a resident. He was a handsome man in his late 20s. "Tell me about your pain," he said. I felt sorry that he had a name like "Toby." Parents are sometimes cruel when they name their children.

I explained how the pain hit me suddenly while walking down Bridgeway. "Did you eat anything funny?" he inquired. "Any exotic Mexican or Italian food?"

"Don't think so. I had a steak for lunch."

A nurse came in with an IV. "We're going to start you on some saline solution and some morphine," said Dr. Pratt.

"Ah the good stuff," I said.

"You'll feel better in just a few minutes."

Julie sat next to me looking extremely concerned and held my hand. "How are you, champ?" she asked.

I yawned and was mercifully starting to drift off from the meds.

"I'm going to order an MRI and see if there's something going on that we can't anticipate." said Pratt. "Right now we need to start eliminating things that it isn't."

Julie became increasingly concerned. "What do you think it might be?" she asked. Pratt shrugged. "I've never seen him so uncomfortable," she added. "I feel so sorry for him."

I woke up when they put me on a gurney and wheeled me to radiology. A young Asian woman named Aimee was the tech on duty. She was a small woman with a big smile and a soft reassuring voice. She asked the orderly who brought me to her to help me move onto the table. The MRI took only a few minutes. They wheeled me back to the room in the ER where Julie was waiting in the hallway and had a worried look on her face.

"Oh, baby, how are you feeling?" she asked.

I gave her a faint smile and drifted back to sleep. Julie held my hand. I woke once again when Toby Pratt re-entered the room. He pulled up a chair and spoke. "Scott, I'm afraid we really don't know what's wrong with you. In the work-up we did when you came in you said that you have had kidney stones in the past. On one of the x-rays I saw what looked like what might be a stone. It takes awhile sometimes to figure out what the problem might actually be."

"Think all of this pain is from one stone?"

"Could be. I just don't know. It all depends how it's positioned in the kidney. I want you to go see you primary care physician, explain what happened, and see what he wants to do. You said he's here at UC. He can pull up my notes online. I'm going to send you home with Vicodin and discharge you."

"Are you sure that's a good idea?" I asked hoping there was some kind of magic bullet that would suddenly make me feel better.

"There's no reason to hold you right now," he replied. "If it gets worse just come back and we'll admit you."

I thanked him for his help. It was almost 4 AM. Julie and I headed over the Golden Gate Bridge for home. The strong pain killers were wearing off. I suddenly was very much awake.

"You're not going to work today," insisted Julie. "You've got to take it easy. One day won't make difference."

"Nah, I'm feeling better. Let's see what happens." She knew I would resist staying home. I just had too much to do.

"Are you hungry?" she asked.

I told her to not worry about it and get some sleep. I would fend for myself.

When we got home she pulled down the hill so I wouldn't have to walk so far. She walked me to the door and let me in. Emma was waiting there and very happy to see me as always.

"I'm going to go jump in the shower," I said. "All I want right now is a nice long hot shower."

The hot water felt good. The pain had mostly subsided. When I got out of the shower and dressed I walked over to the living room and found Julie sleeping on the couch. I went into the kitchen made myself breakfast. I was feeling considerably better. I decided to take a quick nap and then head to the office. This was against my better judgment, but I thought I'd feel better there than sitting around the house watching CNN or MSNBC. Even when I was a kid I resisted staying home from school when I was sick. I always feel better being out and about. I was determined that if I just kept moving sooner or later I might start feeling better. I prided myself as being fairly tough. I had just been through a lot and knew I would make it through this sooner or later. This was a small speed bump.

Two

At the same time Scott Butler was making himself breakfast Sausalito Police Officer Stacey Gordon pulled into the 7-11 for a cup of coffee. She was nearing the end of her shift and needed a jolt of caffeine to make it through the final hour. It had been a quiet night, and she was anxious to get home to see her daughter and catch a few hours of sleep before working part of another shift to get some overtime. She was amazed how little sleep she actually needed, but it sure felt good. Her father used to tell her, "Sleep is for sissies." She wasn't all that sure she agreed with him. Right now she felt like she could sleep for a week. She couldn't remember the last time she felt completely rested.

Her marriage sadly ended several months ago, and she was now a single mom. Her daughter Natasha was her pride and joy. Stacey's ex was a construction worker who had a hard time keeping a job and drank too much, therefore there was no spousal or child support on the table. That was okay. She was determined to show everyone that she could make it on her own. However, she was having a difficult time paying her bills. Her parents were providing some financial assistance, but she hated that. She was grown up, and shouldn't have to be relying on anyone to come to her rescue. She had to do this on her own. She was tired of everyone in her life worrying about her.

Azfar Saajar, who worked most overnight shifts at the 7-11, always offered to buy Stacey coffee and obviously had a crush on her. She always turned him down but was flattered. She wasn't sure why she always refused his offer but thought it was the right thing to do. If she accepted the free java it might send out the wrong message. Stacey was hungry and grabbed a glazed donut. She had just lost 12 pounds from the stress of the divorce and felt she could afford it. She knew she'd get a sugar rush, and that would help keep her alert as well, which was a clever rationalization. For a moment she considered grabbing a second donut but common sense prevailed. She had fought hard to keep her weight under control during a period when many women following a divorce might have eaten themselves into oblivion.

It had been a quiet shift, maybe even too quiet. She wound up giving three speeding tickets, rousted Sausalito's sole homeless person, Stella, out of sleeping in the post office and answered one domestic violence call. Those were the messy ones that she didn't like to go on. It reminded her too much of how her father used to beat her mother. California is a must-arrest state in domestic violence cases. This time she was actually arresting the wife who was highly intoxicated and had broken a wine bottle over her husband's head. Even as she was leading the wife away the two were professing their undying love for each other. They would let her out the next day on her own recognizance, and the fun would start all over again. It was just another strange night in Sausalito. No-one would believe half of the things she wound up doing so she refrained from talking about what went on at work.

She got in her car, headed south on Bridgeway and veered onto Caledonia Street. To have something to do for the last hour rather than riding aimlessly through Sausalito she started checking license plates looking for ones that were expired. On one block alone she found three that were out of date. In front of Smitty's, the redneck bar on the 200 block of Caledonia, a man with a full white beard was sweeping the sidewalk. It looked like it had been quite the night at Smitty's. Stacey regularly answered noise complaints regarding Smitty's and found herself stopping there to quiet everyone down a couple times each week. She didn't have to do too much convincing. Usually just the sight of her pulling up outside did the trick. She hated dealing with noisy drunks, especially women who had too much to drink and wanted to fight her. She could usually handle herself in a physical altercation but a couple times had to call for back-up at Smitty's.

On the next block in front of the movie theater she saw a young couple, bundled up, out for a morning jog. She wondered why anyone would be up at this hour if they absolutely didn't have to. Some of the locals were a bit too gung ho when it came to physical fitness. The couple had dog with them, a yellow lab they called Chester.

She turned her cruiser back on Bridgeway and headed for a final drive through the downtown area. She passed the Casa Madrona Hotel where a lone cab sat out front hoping for a fare to SFO. On the opposite side of the street was a small park. Guarding the park were two gigantic concrete elephants on concrete pedestals, Pee Wee and Jumbo, remnants of the 1915 World's Fair held in San Francisco. As she passed the statues she noticed something or somebody lying on the ground next to one of the elephants.

She parked her cruiser in front of the Wells Fargo Bank and crossed the street. Lying next to the elephant on the left was the body of a man in his mid 40s. He had a bullet in his forehead and a look on his face that begged, "Why?" He wore what appeared to be an expensive suit. She thought it might be an Armani. He also had on an expensive pair of Italian loafers. She had been on the force three years, and this was the first dead body she had found. It didn't unravel her, but she wasn't sure what to do. Homicides were rare in Sausalito.

Stacey took out her cell phone and called her watch commander, Lt. Barry Peterson. He arrived a few minutes later. He was a long lanky man with a bad haircut. He had huge ears and an equally big nose and looked like he was put together with spare parts. Peterson cursed the fact that they found this unlucky guy right at the end of the shift. This meant at least three more hours on duty and a pile of paperwork.

Peterson called the Marin County Sheriff's Police and asked that they send out a CSI unit. The dispatcher had to roust these people out of a warm bed so it took about an hour for them to arrive. The Marin Coroner's office was called to come and stand by to remove the body once CSI was done with the crime scene. While waiting for the CSI unit they taped off the area. A Marin County Sheriff's Police cruiser pulled up several minutes later and two officers got out, a man and a portly woman. They approached the Sausalito officers clearly unhappy that they were there.

"How are you guys?" asked Peterson trying to sound cheery. He always hated when he had to rely on someone from Marin County. He felt they always acted as if they knew so much more than the Sausalito cops and that they were doing them a big favor just by showing up. However, there was no reason to act snarky and piss them off.

"We're about as happy as you are that we're right about against shift change and you stumbled across this poor guy," said the woman deputy from the sheriff's Police.

Peterson laughed. Gordon explained how she had found the body and there was no immediate explanation how or why it was there. She attempted to explain her discovery in more detail, but the Marin Police were clearly uninterested.

About two hours and several cups of coffee later the CSI team finished their work and said it was okay to remove the body. The ambulance from the coroner arrived minutes later and took the body to the morgue in San Rafael, the county seat. Stacey Gordon couldn't stop thinking about the victim. Who was this person? Did he have anyone who loved him that wouldn't know he was dead? How did this happen to him? The gunshot wound was done with great precision. It had not been part of a robbery. The man still had his wallet filled with almost three hundred dollars in cash. However, all ID, driver's license, credit cards etc. had been removed. It had been a hit, but a hit in Sausalito? Things like that weren't supposed to happen in Sausalito. It was after all an artist's colony. How strange! It had been seven years since the last murder in this picturesque little town on the Bay. The next day the residents of Sausalito would be in shock because of what happened the night before.

Stacey got back in her cruiser, made a u-turn and headed back to the Police station. She was tired and desperately wanted to get home to make her daughter breakfast and drive her to school. She called her sister who stayed with Stacey's daughter each night and told her what has transpired. "I'm going to be at the station till least 10 AM," she moaned. "Then I've got to be back here a few hours later. Can you please take Natasha to school?"

Her sister told her to not worry about a thing. Stacey parked her car in the closest space to the door of the temporary building that served as the Police station and entered. It had been the temporary home for going on 20 years, and the city had recently broken ground on a new combination Police and fire station which would make things both more efficient and pleasant. She said good morning to Gayle, the dispatcher, and sat down in the meeting room to start filling out the paperwork, a task she dreaded. She briefly got up, grabbed a cup of stale coffee and returned to the task at hand.

She figured it would take almost three hours to complete all the forms. Several minutes later Barry Peterson entered the room. "Do you need some help?" he asked. She assured him that she was just fine and didn't need any help. He said he was grateful and went home. Although she could have used the help Peterson was starting to get on her nerves and she thought it was better to plod through it on her own rather than endure three hours in the same room as Peterson.

The sun was now rising in Sausalito. The city was waking up and preparing for another day. The Winship Restaurant near Gabrielsen Park was opening its doors. It was a favorite of East Coast visitors who were up early because of the three hour time difference and were glad to find a place open early for breakfast. The food at the Winship was good, not great but reliable. The service was friendly and accommodating.

A black Lincoln Town Car made its way over the Golden Gate Bridge and took the first exit, Alexander, and headed down the long winding road into Sausalito. At this time of the morning there were very few cars on the street. A truck carrying produce was headed for the Golden Gate Market, a small corner store on the edge of Downtown Sausalito. The truck was going under the speed limit which frustrated the driver of the black limo. When the truck turned into the parking lot of the market, the limo accelerated and now found itself driving along Richardson Bay. There were few other cars on the road. The traffic was punctuated by an occasional zealot out for a morning ride on his bike. The waters of the Bay were calm.

Moments later the Town Car came to the giant concrete elephants proudly guarding the park. The car slowed as it passed the park and momentarily stopped. The man in the back seat rolled down his tinted window, took a peek and dialed his cell phone. When the person on the other end answered the man simply said, "The body is gone." The car sped up and drove away. The man in the back seat smiled. The deed had been done. He hated loose ends. Justice had been served. A powerful message had been sent.

Three

I was determined to go to the office after having breakfast, but it didn't quite work out that way. I sat down for a minute in my favorite chair, closed my eyes and immediately fell asleep. I woke up at 11AM when I heard Julie enter the shower. Although I was tempted to join her I decided to grab a few extra minutes of shut eye.

Julie gave me a kiss on the forehead. I opened my eyes and smiled.

"How are you feeling?" she asked. "You had a rough night."

"Feeling better. I'm going to get ready and walk to the office."

"Are you sure?" I'll be happy to drive you. You don't want to over do it."

"I'm sure." I was in denial that there actually might be something wrong with me.

I went into the bathroom, looked in the mirror and didn't like what I saw. I looked old. Maybe I was just tired. I wondered what I could do to help myself. My hair was starting to turn grey. That bothered me. I wondered whether or not I should start coloring it. I suggested that to Julie one time, and all I got was a polite laugh and a knowing smile. I decided not to for the time being. I noticed some wrinkles around my eyes. I put on my best suit so at least I looked successful and somewhat youthful and walked down Bridgeway to my office.

When I got there I found a client waiting for me. Her name was Bernice Stava. She has lived in Sausalito for almost 50 years and her view was in jeopardy. Sausalito residents are very protective of their views. Her neighbor across the street was building up and adding a second story on their home. It blocked a tiny part of Bernice's view. The city has been more than happy to issue a permit for the work, and the city council easily dismissed her appeal. She was in such angst, and I wasn't sure what, if anything, we could do. Before she left she gave me a tin full of cookies she made the night before. I was very moved.

"Bernice, you are the sweetest woman," I said. "Thank you." She gave me a peck on the cheek and headed towards the door. I walked her down the stairs. As I started back up the stairs the pain hit again, this time even more severe than before. I sat down on the stairs and grabbed my side.

"Oh, shit," I said. "Why in the world is this happening to me?" Several minutes later the pain subsided. I walked up the rest of the stairs and sat down at my desk. The pain hit again. I decided to call my doctor, Josh Asher, at UCSF. His office manager, a woman named Rosa answered the phone. I explained my pain and that this was an on-going problem.

"Where does it hurt, Scott?" she asked.

"In my stomach, just to the right of center."

"Scott, do you want to see Josh or go to the ER?"

"Let's start with Josh."

"Can you be here at 2.PM? He can see you then. But be on time. He's got a really full schedule."

I told her I would be there and called Julie who said she would drive me and to be out front at one o'clock. That was more than an hour away. I lay down on the couch in my office, but the pain persisted. I had time to walk over to Poggio and get something to eat, but I had absolutely no appetite. The phone rang. I answered it and found my Dad on the other end. He had just turned 80 and was in great shape. He played golf almost every day, and I was jealous. I was tempted to tell him about my pain but decided not to. Why worry an old man?

We had the conversation every time we spoke.

"How's the weather, Dad?" He was in Chicago.

"Not as nice as by you I bet."

"How do you feel?

"Not bad for an old guy," he laughed. This was the same answer to this question every time I asked. I politely laughed back.

"How's Mom? What's she been up to?"

"She's out having lunch with her friends," he said sounding relieved he had some time by himself. After all these years they still enjoyed each other's company but sometimes familiarity breeds contempt.

We talked for another ten minutes about the Chicago White Sox, my brother's sudden good fortune, and anything else that was on his mind. I felt bad if I didn't call my Dad every few days.

"Give Mom a hug for me," I asked. "I've got to go." We agreed to talk again soon. I always felt better after talking to my Dad. Even though we've had our problems, he was still one of my best friends.

I decided to go out front and wait for Julie. I knew she'd be early, and she was already waiting for me. She gave me a peck on the cheek and headed down Bridgeway towards UCSF. Traffic was mild. She had a heavy look of concern on her face.

"You poor dear," she said. "How does it feel?"

"It hurts like hell."

It took about 25 minutes to get across the Golden Gate Bridge and into the garage underneath the medical office building at 350 Parnassus. Julie found a parking place on the fourth level near the elevator. She was surprised as it was usually next to impossible to find a place to park at the medical center.

We took the elevator up to the first floor where Josh Asher had his office. Rosa took me into an exam room as soon as I walked in the door. She asked Julie to have a seat in the waiting room. Julie was disappointed. She wanted to come in the exam room with me. "Relax," I told her. "We'll call you in soon."

Josh Asher was a slight man a few years younger than me. He had a meteoric rise at UCSF and was now Associate Chief of Staff and in charge of all outpatient care. He liked seeing patients and still maintained a small practice. He operated out of the Executive Health Service. He came to the medical center 15 years ago after medical school at UCLA and his residency at Johns Hopkins in Baltimore. He was caring, and he was smart. Patients loved him. He was wise, and he was thorough. Best of all he always looked like he really cared. Josh had a calm demeanor that gave you confidence. Even in the darkest moment he was a ray of sunshine.

"Hi, Scott," he said. "I understand we have a problem. Tell me about it." He wasn't one to waste time on small talk.

I showed him where it hurt. "I can't remember ever having this kind of pain," I said. "It hurts like hell." He had me lie down and lower my pants. He probed my abdomen. When he hit the spot on my right I cried out.

"There was nothing conclusive on the MRI when you came to the ER last night," he said. He probed my stomach. He touched a spot that made the pain even worse. "Scott," he continued, "I'm going to admit you for some tests. This could be any number of different things. We have to start eliminating possibilities."

I offered no resistance. He called Julie in and explained what he was going to do. She looked very concerned. "It's just some routine tests," he told her. "Nothing much to worry about." But he was worried, and so was I.

• • •

Rosa called admitting and worked her magic so I didn't to go through the ordeal of waiting in line in the hospital lobby to be admitted. Several minutes later an orderly in green scrubs came over with a wheel chair to take me across the street to the hospital. We briefly stopped at admitting and found my room assignment. He wheeled me up to a private room on the sixth floor. I was asked to change into a hospital gown, which I did and climbed into bed. A few minutes later a nurse named Brenda Taylor came in and introduced herself. She was a stern looking woman who looked like she hadn't smiled since she was a child. However, she looked serious and competent. Right now I would rather have excellent medical care than a new friend.

"Mr. Butler," she said, "Dr. Asher has ordered a series of tests. It's getting late. All we're going to do today is draw some blood. We'll do the rest tomorrow." I was disappointed   I would have preferred they would do tests right then and there.

Julie appeared a few minutes later. She wanted to spend the night. I told her to go home. "Are you sure?" she asked. She protested, but I prevailed.

"I'm sure. All I want to do is get some sleep. Come back in the morning." She said she would. She gave me a kiss on the cheek and said "I love you," as she left.

Minutes later a phlebotomist named Heather entered my room and explained what she was going to do. She took three vials of blood and wished me good luck. Josh Asher entered my room as she was leaving. He had a concerned look on his face.

"Hey, Scott, I wanted to let you know what we're going to be looking at. This young woman just drew some blood for a CBC, which will allow us to take a peek at all sorts of things dealing with your blood."

He went on to tell me that they would draw some more blood the next morning, tests called amylase and hpase to test my pancreatic enzymes. He also ordered a series of liver function tests. "If you're feeling any better tomorrow I'll let you go home," he said.

I told him I was still in a considerable amount of pain. He ordered a pain pump that I would be able to activate and give me a jolt of morphine whenever I needed it. A nurse brought it in about 20 minutes later and showed me how to use it. Minutes after giving myself the first dose I was out like a light.

My sleep was interrupted a couple hours later by a well-meaning male nurse who was assigned to me that night and came in to take my blood pressure. As I woke my pain intensified so I gave myself another helping of morphine. This time sleep didn't come so easily. I had a lot on my mind. Plus it was a busy night in the hospital, and every few minutes someone was being paged. A hospital is not a quiet place at night. I eventually fell back asleep and slept through the next blood pressure Check.

Julie arrived home dead tired. She was worried about Scott and all she wanted to do was crawl into bed. She found a package for Scott waiting on the porch by the door. She brought it in and put it on his desk, Emma was waiting at the front door doing the little dance she did when she really had to go out and pee. Julie grabbed Emma's leash and took her out in the yard in the back by the lawn. Emma showed no immediate interest in relieving herself and finally walked behind a bush, did her thing and headed back towards the house.

• • •

The phone rang as she entered the house. She thought it might be Scott. She heard heavy breathing and then a hang-up on the other end. She hit *69 on her phone and heard the recording that the number that called her was a private number, and the number was not traceable.

She lay down on the couch and woke up at 7 AM when the garbage man came, and Emma announced the arrival by barking. Julie called the hospital; Scott answered on the third ring. He said he was being discharged at 11 AM. Julie promised to be there to drive him home

Stacey Gordon was playing with her daughter when the phone rang. She was afraid to answer the phone. She feared it was someone at the station. She answered the phone and found indeed it was Barry Peterson who sounded apologetic for calling. "Stacey," he said, "I'm so sorry to be calling you on your day off. Could you please come down to the station?"
"What's up?" she asked.

"Special Agent Toland from the San Francisco office of the FBI is here. It has to do with the body you found by the elephant."

"Let me see if I can get someone to watch my little girl."

She called everyone on her list and kept getting turn downs. Finally Emily Zimney, a neighbor in her late 70s agreed to stay with Natasha. "It shouldn't be more than a couple hours." She arrived about fifteen minutes later. She had made coffee for her neighbor. It took Stacey ten minutes to drive to the station. When she got there she found Barry Peterson and Chief Doug Herrmann in the conference room meeting with Special Agent John Toland. After introductions were made Barry Peterson spoke. "Thanks for coming in, Stacey. I'm sorry we had to tear you away from your daughter."

"That's okay," she replied. "You know you can always count on me."

"Stacey, we need your help," said Toland. "We were able to identify the victim. His name is Vincent Check, a small time hood and member of the Manfredo family of Chicago."

"What's he doing in San Francisco? Who do you believe put out the hit?"

"We have no idea," said Toland. "However, we did find one thing very disturbing, a list in his pocket of several prominent people in Sausalito along with their phone numbers."

"What do you think that's all about?" she asked.

"We don't know," said Chief Herrmann. "I'd like you to work with Special Agent Toland to find out what this is all about. Needless to say, this is very sensitive and must remain very confidential. This list is a who's who of the upper echelon in Sausalito. Once they know what we have found there will be a lot of very upset people. We're messing with the movers and shakers. These are the people who could actually cost me my job, but we've got to do the right thing."

"I understand," she replied. "Of course I will do whatever I can to help."

They showed her the list:

Mike Long, Mayor

Howie Steiner, City Council member
Loretta Connelly, City Council member
John Patterson, Assistant City Attorney
Jim Squires, Chairman of the planning commission
Sid Emmett, Publisher of the local newspaper, the .Marin Times
Rhonda Shankland, local realtor

The group discussed the list and what it possibly could mean. "These are very high profile people in Sausalito," cautioned Peterson. "We need to find out why these names were in his pocket. That may tell us why the deceased is no longer with us. I want you to lead the investigation."

"Why me?"

Chief Herrmann jumped in, "If one of us starts fishing around looking for answers it's going to set off alarms with these people. You are every bit as good as anyone of us. You're the right person for the job." She mildly protested but was grateful for the opportunity. She was flattered that they were showing so much confidence in her. She thought this might actually be the greatest challenge of her still young career. This could either make or break her future,

She thanked them for the confidence and spent another half hour with Toland. He explained that they had been watching the victim, Vincent Check, for some time and explained more about his involvement with organized crime. He also gave her a very thick confidential file that went into great deal about Check's past.

Stacey paused and spoke. "I've got to ask you again. Why in the world does the FBI want to work with me on this investigation? Isn't this something you would rather handle on your own? I'm still trying to absorb what you've asked me to do."

"Look, Stacey. Every investigation is different. When we're working on a case in a small town like Sausalito it's not unusual for us to team with the local police. We're going to get a lot farther keeping the initial part of the investigation low key. If word gets out that the FBI is involved all of the people on that list will very quickly lawyer up, and it will be very difficult to get anything done. I personally have known about you for some time. It's our job to also know what talent is out there in the field. You are up for the task. This will advance your career and give you the opportunity to do things other than writing traffic tickets and answering domestic violence calls. You are the right person for this job. If you need help all you've got to do is ask."

It was shortly after midnight. The man parked his nondescript car in the parking lot behind City Hall. He looked around and made sure no-one was watching. He walked down the steps, fumbled for his keys and opened the back door. He quietly walked down the hall and once again grabbed his keys and opened the door to his office. He opened up a file drawer, the second from the top, and took out a large file folder. He locked up his office and the building and returned to his car. A Police cruiser, one of four that was on patrol during the night, passed by. He prayed the car didn't stop by. It didn't. He climbed back in his car, headed down the hill, and made a right turn on Bridgeway. He was back at home before anyone noticed he was gone.

● ○ ●

He placed the folder on the desk in his home office. The label on the file read, "Vincent Check." He sat back in his desk chair, closed his eyes and sighed; He went over to a neighboring cabinet and took out a bottle of Jack Daniels. He put in some ice from the ever full ice bucket and poured himself a drink. Things were getting more interesting.

Four

It was 7:30 .PM, and a group of 17 men and women had gathered in the basement of St. Mary Star of the Sea Church in Sausalito. The church sat high on a hill overlooking Richardson Bay. Its history corresponds with that of the city itself and dates back to the 1850s.

The group met every Monday, Wednesday, and Friday evening come hell or high water. The group was usually made up of the same people every meeting with a new person or two drifting in and out every once in a while. The group typically started convening a little after 7 .PM. The first person to arrive put the folding chairs in a circle and set out various pieces of inspirational literature. It was a Gamblers Anonymous meeting, and everyone was on a first name only basis. Everything that happened in a meeting truly stayed there. It was a model similar to AA. .

They took turns being leader. That night a petite woman in her 30s named Trudy was leader. It wasn't necessarily her turn, but she was the first person to show up and gained the honor by default. At precisely 7:30 .PM she called the meeting to order and welcomed everyone. They stood, held hands, and said the serenity prayer. They then went around the circle for every person to introduce himself or herself. Everyone was strictly on a first name basis. If they bumped into each other on the street they were not to discuss being at the meetings together.

The first person was a portly man named Ralph. He stood and spoke. "My name is Ralph, and I'm an addict."

The group responded, "Hello, Ralph."

The second person was a meek looking woman named Rhoda. She was tearing up as she spoke, "My name is Rhoda, and I'm an addict."

"Hello, Rhoda."

The third person was a surfer dude type named Kyle. "Good evening, my name is Kyle, and I'm an addict."

"Hello, Kyle."

"Hello everyone, my name is Scott, and I'm an addict."

I got to the office early Thursday morning. I didn't sleep well the night before. I had a lot on my mind. The situation with the Alta Mira was a mess. Also I hadn't heard from Josh Asher's office in a while. I had been waiting for the results of my test to come back. I had been resisting calling. I guess I was afraid what I was going to find out. I looked up the phone number of the Executive Health Service at UCSF and starting dialing about six times. It was shortly before 11 AM. I finally got up the courage and called. Rosa answered the phone.

"Hello, Scott," she said. "What can I do for you?"

"Rosa, I was hoping the results of my tests were back," I said. "Would you see what you can find out please?"

"Just a minute Scott, let me see what I can pull up on the computer." There was a long period of silence.

"Are you still there, Rosa?" I asked.

"Scott, I'm afraid I can't give you the results. A doctor has to do so."

"Okay, where's Josh?"

"He's giving a seminar at the Cleveland Clinic."

"Okay, is there another doctor around?"

"Josh really should talk to you."

"Rosa, it sounds like something's wrong. If there wasn't anything wrong you'd tell me."

"Josh I can't tell you anything more."

"I'm sure if everything was fine you'd tell me not to worry."

"He's back Monday."

"Rosa, this will drive me crazy. I want to know what's up today. I'm a big boy. I can take it. Give me the number of his hotel in Cleveland. I can't wait till Monday. I need to speak with someone now."

"Scott, I will try to find someone to call you." She said sounding irritated. "You've got to understand everyone is very busy."

"When will I hear from someone? Come on, Rosa. You've got to help me."

"As soon as I can find someone I will have them call you." Click.
Thirty minutes later there was no response. I called Rosa again. She sounded more irritated. "I'll be right back." I held on for six minutes, the longest six minutes of my life. She came back. "Scott, this is Dr. Wishani, an internist in the faculty internal medicine practice."

"Hello, Mr. Butler," he said. I told him "Scott" was fine." "Okay, Scott," he continued. "This is the hardest part of any doctor's job. The tests are quite clear. You have a large mass on your pancreas. A mass of this size is malignant 99 percent of the time. The cancer spreads very quickly."

"Don't you need to do a biopsy?" My life was starting to flash in front of my eyes.

"Scott, we don't. You're certainly welcome to get a second opinion if you like, but someone else will tell you exactly the same thing. We'll do everything we can to keep you comfortable."

"What are you telling me?"

"It's time to start getting your affairs in order. This is a very aggressive cancer."

I felt like I had been hit in the head with a baseball bat. I didn't know whether to cry or be pissed.

"What...what are you telling me?"

"This is terminal. Scott. I AM deeply sorry." I doubted he was sorry. "I'm going to give you back to Rosa. She'll set up an appointment for you to see Dr. Asher."

"Scott, I don't know what to say," she said.

"When can I see Josh?" I whispered. She told me to be there the day after tomorrow at 10 AM. I said, "Thank you" and hung up the phone. It's a surreal moment when you're told you're dying. Nothing prepares you for it. I sat there close to an hour and stared out the window. I didn't know what to do. I wondered how I would tell Julie. What would I say? What would I do to ease her pain? How would I tell my parents? How would I tell my brother? What would I do with the time I had left? You always wondered how you would handle a moment like this, and I had no idea. This was all so hard to comprehend.

I locked my office and walked down to where the ferry docked and watched crowds of tourists get onboard for their trip back to the Ferry Building in San Francisco. I envied them. They looked happy. I decided to walk over to Julie's shop and take her to lunch. I was determined to stay strong. One of us had to be okay to help the other.

I slowly walked down Caledonia Street towards her shop. I was in no hurry to get there. Strangely enough I felt the best I did in a long time. When I walked in the front door she looked both happy and surprised to see me. She was taking care of two customers, a mother and daughter who were picking out needlepoint for a project they wanted to work on together. Julie patiently showed them different alternatives. They eventually found something they like, paid, thanked Julie for her help and left.

"What are you doing here?" she asked. "I thought you were so busy today."

"I just thought it would be nice to take you to lunch."

She smiled and put a sign in the window that read "I'll be back soon. Please come back." "We don't need to hurry," she said. "It's been really slow today. That Mom and her daughter were the only customers I've had all day."

We decided to go to Café Da Vino about four blocks down Caledonia Street. It was a small Italian restaurant that we both liked and frequented at least a couple times each month. I held her hand as we walked down the street. I tried to imagine how she would handle being on her own. I was glad I had some time to pull things together so she wouldn't have to worry about financial matters. There were so many things I needed to do in the time we had left. As long as we had been together we had wanted to visit Italy but had never gotten there. I decided we had to go. I wanted to give her some memories to help her through the inevitable.

When we got to the restaurant our friend, Elizabeth, the restaurant's manager greeted us and said "The restaurant was half empty. "Sit any place you like," she said. I grabbed a table in the back. I wanted a nice private place to break the news. For a moment I debated whether or not to tell her yet. Should I spare her the pain for a while? I decided she needed to know. I had to tell her now. If it were the other way around I would want to know.

We looked at our menus and ordered. My eyes started to well with tears.

"What's wrong, Scott," she asked. "Are your folks okay?"

"They're okay, but I'm not."
"What are you trying to tell me?" she pleaded.

"The results came back from my tests…"It was hard to finish.

"What did you find out, Scott? Please tell me."
"They found a mass on my pancreas. It's spreading quickly. There's not much they can do. I AM so sorry." I fought back tears.

"Scott, what are you apologizing for? We'll fight this. You're in good hands."

"Juls, there's nothing they can do."

"What do you mean?"
"Juls, pancreatic cancer spreads quickly. The mortality rate is almost 100%. I'm going to see Josh on Monday. I don't know what to do. I seem to be always come up with an answer. This time I can't save myself."

Julie started to quietly weep. They brought out our food. We shoved it to the side She grabbed my hand. We sat there saying nothing for over an hour.

A group six men sat in a room in the back of a dark restaurant in North Beach, the Italian section of San Francisco. Each man had a very serious look on his face and wore a dark suit.

One man spoke," Shouldn't we get on with this?" he asked.

A large man with a half filled plate of Lasagna spoke. "Not so fast. I'm not done eating. Finish your food too and then we'll talk." The first man did what he was told. About ten minutes later the large man spoke once again. "Okay, I'm ready."

The other men were still eating but put down their forks and listened attentively. Then the large man spoke again. "We had a serious problem I believe you all know," he said sternly. "We'd been betrayed by one of our own "The men around the table shook their heads in agreement.

"We had to do something about it. It was the right thing to do."

The men shook their heads in agreement.

The large man said, "That little prick betrayed us."

Five

Stacey Gordon stayed at the station after her shift. She wanted some quiet time which she couldn't get at home. She had been given the assignment of trying to figure out the strange case of Vincent Check. She had thought of asking the Chief to relieve her of patrol duty for a while as she worked on the list but decided that would blow the secret. Only four people, including Stacey knew about the list, and that was the way it had to be. She wished she could call on others in the department for advice and counsel but knew that could not be the case. She was working on this independently.

She grabbed a yellow legal pad and started writing the names that were on the list in Vincent Check's pocket when he was found dead as a door nail at the feet of Pee Wee, the giant concrete elephant in Downtown Sausalito. She personally knew of everyone on the list, some better than others, and jotted random notes next to each name. Later she would try to figure out how the names on the list were connected and what in the world they were doing on a list in the deceased's coat pocket.

The List:
Mike Long, Mayor

- On the city council longer than anyone who like to remember.

- Arrogant
- Not necessarily the brightest guy in the world
- Long time Sausalito resident
- Drinks too much

Howie Steiner, City council member
- Dumb as dirt
- How did this guy ever get elected?
- Used to own the car wash and gas station
- Excellent schmoozer.

Loretta Connelly, City Council member
- Moved to Sausalito about four years ago
- Quiet
- Probably the smartest person on the city council
- Recently widowed
- Very wealthy
- Trust fund

John Patterson, City Attorney
- Delusions of adequacy
- Loud and obnoxious
- Viper

Jim Squires, Chairman planning commission
- Classic nice guy
- Very involved with various city activities
- Considered very fair

Sid Emmett, newspaper publisher
- Thinks he's more important than he is

- The last guy in the world you want to run afoul
- Also loud and obnoxious
- Bad temper

Rhonda Shankland
- Dates Sid Emmett
- Both respected and feared

Stacey sat and stared at her notes. Nothing jumped off the page as to what this list was all about. She would continue her work. Unfortunately other than the chief she had no-one to consult with. She knew that one way or another she would find the chutzpah to get this done.

At approximately 6AM a call came into the San Francisco Police station on Fillmore Street. It was a non-descript grey building built in the late 1960s. It was located in an area called, "The Western Addition," the highest crime area in the city. On the other end of the phone was a woman who identified herself as Irene Shaw. She told the dispatcher that she had better send an officer. She had been walking her dog in the park and found a body. It was the body of a young man, probably in his mid 30s. The man had met his untimely demise with a bullet in the middle of his forehead. Officers Dwayne Kiley and Ronnie Lee were first to arrive. The CSI unit arrived minutes later. It was the 87th homicide that year for the city of San Francisco. It was an efficient mob hit. There was no clear indication why this man had been murdered.

Six

Julie insisted on going to see Josh with me. I tried to talk her out of it, but she wouldn't agree to stay behind. I actually was glad she was going with me. Everything I read said take with someone when you go see your doctor to discuss what to do with your cancer. I guess the theory is you're so emotional when you go see your doctor that someone should be there with you who will be able to comprehend and remember what the doctor had to say. As cool that I was in the court room I knew I had never faced anything quite like this in the past.

We pulled into the garage at UCSF about 15 minutes before my scheduled appointment. There's a Starbucks in the lobby of the 350 Parnasus building where Josh Asher's office was located. We had time to grab a latte before heading through the door behind Starbuck's for my appointment. Rosa was sitting at her desk by the door and told us to have a seat. She'd tell Josh we were there. We had to wait only about five minutes before Josh emerged from an exAM room and told us to come in. Josh is a good looking young doctor, and Julie was impressed. I had forgotten she had never met him before. He offered us chairs in front of his desk, pulled his chair out from behind his desk and sat with us. Julie looked like she was going to pass out. Suddenly I felt worse for her than I did for myself.

"I can only guess how difficult this is for both of you," he said. "I want to explain what we believe is going on and what we're going to do about it." He turned around his computer and called up my test results. The first screen we looked at was my CT scan. "Here's the problem," he said pointing to the mass. "Pancreatic cancer grows with lightning speed. A tumor of this size is typically always cancer. You have what is known as pancreatic adenocarcinoma. It's among the most aggressive of all cancers. As was the case with you by the time it's diagnosed it has already spread to the most distant points of the body. Unfortunately it's also very resistant to any kind of medical treatment.

"Always?" I asked.

"I've never see one that wasn't. But that doesn't mean we shouldn't try everything possible. Miracles happen."

He went on to explain that there was a clinical trial in progress that he possibly could me into. "You never know what kind of results you get from one of these studies," he continued.

"But rarely does anything really work," I said.

"Not necessarily. I AM also going to refer you to an oncologist here at UC, Tom O'Leary. We need all the smart people we can get on our team. He's the kind of guy I would refer my Dad or brother to."

He gave me a prescription for some pain meds. "You're going to need these sooner than later." He also told me to come back in a month. Julie asked how much time I had left. "We never like to put a timeline on an illness. We never give up. We never stop trying. We never give up hope and neither should you. All I would advise you right now is to start tying together any small details of your life. I guess this is something we should all do. No matter what happens, we will always do whatever we can to minimize your suffering."

I knew he had given us the politically correct comments you give someone who is dying, Julie seemed to take some comfort in what Josh had said. I knew better. Josh gave both of us a hug. We left his office, rode the elevator down to the garage, paid and left the garage, and drove back to Sausalito without saying a word. There wasn't much to be said. We were both in shock and somehow trying to comfort each other.

When we arrived home Julie spoke. "How are you, sweetheart?"

"It's strange I actually feel fine."

"We're going to fight this, Scott. We're not going to give up. We need to absorb everything that's happened and move on from there."

"I know," I said softly. I gave her a kiss. "I'm going to the office."

"Why?" she asked. "Why don't you just stay home? What's so important at the office?"

"Because I'm not ready to sit around watching TV and wait to die. There are a lot of things I still need to do."

She looked at me and smiled. She knew exactly what I was talking about. I needed time to absorb everything that was happening to me. I was operating on complete overload. I didn't know whether to laugh or cry or just be angry.

Seven

Everyone has a nasty little secret. I have several. I'm a recovering gambling addict. I used to bet on just about everything imaginable from betting on games to betting on the Oscars to betting on dog fights. It had gotten to the point when Julie had enough. We almost lost our house, and she left me and moved in with a friend in Tiburon. I fought hard to win her back, and it wasn't easy. We went to couple's counseling twice a week for six months. I was miserable living alone and only saw her and spoke with her during these sessions. Six months into therapy she said she'd give me another chance. I would have to agree to go to Gamblers Anonymous meetings each week and to continue in individual therapy. At this point I would have agreed to do anything she wanted me to do.

When she moved back I got banished the guest bedroom. This was hard for me to take. I looked forward to having her warm body next to mine in bed. I looked forward to making love, but she wouldn't even think of that yet. I was just so happy to have her back with me that I dared not to argue. Eventually things got back to normal. We fought constantly, but it was good to let off steam and to put all the cards on the table. Julie was the only woman I had ever loved, and I was determined to hold on to her.

I placed my bets through a woman named Kashi. She had long dread locks and was a very efficient bookie. Any time I wanted to place a bet I would call Kashi, and she would show up wherever I wanted to meet her. She had a cheery disposition and was always glad to take my money. It started out with betting on a college or NFL game every now and then and then escalated to placing a bet just about every day. I got into a bad losing streak and everything I touched over a two- month period turned to crap. I wound up with a gambling debt of over $400,000. I didn't know it at first but later found out that Kashi was working for the mob. Owing that much money was bad. Owing that much money to the mob was terrible beyond belief.

Their collection attempts at first were quiet. Kashi would hunt me down and gently remind me. Then suddenly things got worse. One night when Julie was out of town visiting her folks three large men showed up at my door. I was tempted not to answer, but I knew one of the men had seen me through the living room window.

"Hello, Scott," said the largest of the three men. He was easily 6'6" and must have weighed close to 350 pounds. I quickly decided he was not someone I wanted to mess with.

"Do I know you guys?" I asked. I had an idea whom they actually might be.

"Not us," the same man replied, "but you know of the man we work for." I knew I was in trouble. I tried to stay calm, but it wasn't working. I started sweating profusely.

"Scott, there's a little matter about the $400,000 you owe our boss." I didn't say a word. "Just how do you expect to repay him? He's very unhappy with you and wants us to do something to catch your attention."

"I'll figure something out," I said. "I'll start making payments." I was grasping for straws. I didn't know what to say. I normally stay really cool in the face of adversity. This time I started to visualize my own funeral. Please don't hurt me. I'll borrow the money. I'll think of something. I'm sure my father would be able to help."

"That's not going to work. He's very upset."

I said nothing. I was frozen with fear. We went back and forth for almost an hour, me throwing out ideas, and he rejecting them. After a prolonged period of silence the man spoke.

"Scott, we have a proposition for you."

"What? Anything?"

"We have the need for someone to act as an intermediary when someone wants to put a hit out on someone."

"What? I don't understand."

"You heard me. We provide a service for a fee."

"So if someone wants to put a hit on someone else you provide that service."

"Precisely and it's a great revenue stream," he said with a sadistic smile. "It's a nice little business."

I was amazed how he was casually describing killing people as a business.

"So here's how it goes, Scott. When someone wants to send someone to meet his maker they come to you. You collect some basic information on the intended victim along with recent photos. You then transmit all of the information to the person who's going to do the deed. You do this electronically. You never know who you're sending the hit to. The assassin never knows who's sending it. You then deposit the money in our bank account. You take on this responsibility, Scott, and we'll forgive the $400,000. We'll also give you $5,000 for each transaction you arrange."

"Scott, we know Julie is visiting her parents in LA. We have a man sitting outside their house. If you refuse our generous offer he will kill all three of them." Fear overtook my body. I reluctantly agreed to their offer. I had no choice. Part of the deal was I could tell no one about this arrangement, not even Julie. That would be tough since we told each other everything. We had no secrets. "Scott, if you ever decide not to do this anymore we'll kill them and you as well. Hey, look at it this way, it's a second job." He smiled a big toothy smile. I wanted to vomit. I just wanted them to leave. My heart was beating fast, very fast. I was fearful I would have a heart attack.

They told me they would be in touch soon. They left, and I immediately called Julie to tell her I loved her. The texture of my entire life had suddenly changed. Things would never be the same. My life as I had known it was suddenly over.

Stacey Gordon was getting discouraged. She was still trying to piece together the list of Sausalito luminaries that was found in Vincent Check's pocket but nothing was coming into focus. She was tempted to call everyone on the list and say, "Hey, you may not be aware that your name was on a list found in the pocket of the victim of the hit that was found by the concrete elephants. Any idea why your name was on the list?" Of course she knew this would never fly.

She was getting ready to tell the chief that she was getting nowhere. She decided to give it a few more weeks. Stacey had one more idea she wanted to try. Stacey was tenacious and never gave up on anything even sometimes when she probably should have done so. She was determined to help solve this puzzle. She figured that everyone on the list had already met to make sure they were all saying the same thing if they made the mistake of talking in the first place, If she was not able to move the investigation along in the near future, she would have to become more aggressive. If she didn't, they would stonewall this forever. She thought if she could get just one of the people on the list to talk the others would fall into place.

Eight

Three days after my late night visit from the three scary guys they showed up again, this time at my office with a fourth guy they introduced as Freddie, the computer geek. They told me to lock the office door. "We're going to be here for awhile," said the largest man. "Freddie is going to install a special program on your computer." Freddie was in his mid-20s, dressed poorly, and actually had a pocket protector filled to the brim with pens in his pocket.

"A special program?" I asked.

"Yeah, when someone comes to you wanting our services you will send out the request via an encrypted email program."

"Who am I sending the request to?"

"The beauty about this program is that you will never know. It's easier that way."

"Okay," I said politely. I knew I had no choice. I decided to be quiet. Let them do their thing, and get out of my office as soon as possible.

"The client will give you a cashier's check for $40,000 made out to a name we will create for you. After they leave you will go to the West America Bank branch in Mill Valley where you will open an account in this new name today and deposit the check. We'll give you a great-looking fake ID. Two days later you'll wire it to an off-shore account."

"Sounds so sinister," I said. No-one laughed.

Freddie finished installing the program. It was quite easy. I get the information about the victim from the client, fill out the online form and send it to the person who will "do the deed." It was hard for me to say or think "murder."

So here's what the form looked like. I will fill it in with the help of the client.

- Name
- Age
- Physical Description
- Home Address
- Occupation
- Business Address
- Normal Work Hours
- Favorite Restaurants/Clubs
- Other Places Victim Frequents
- Upload Photos

In other words, this list made it easy to find the victim and complete "the assignment." I felt ill. I couldn't figure out I could ever pull this off. However, I had no choice. My life changed on this day to an extent that I knew I could never get it back and be the man I had been before. I wanted to tell Julie but knew I couldn't. We told each other everything, but I knew it was better if she didn't know. This was a dirty little secret I would have to learn to live with. It wouldn't be easy. I prayed that no one would ever want to put a hit on someone I knew. I somehow knew that wouldn't be the case and wondered how I would handle it when the time came. At the end of the day I was just as guilty of the murder as was the assassin.

Nine

I was feeling pretty good but was obsessed thinking about my illness. How long would I live? What would it feel like when my health started to fail? What kind of pain would I be in? What would the doctors give me to ease my pain? Would I be alert or would I be in a dreamy funk? I had a difficult time using the word, "cancer." I guess to some degree I was still in denial. Being sick was all so new and foreign to me.

Late one morning I got up the courage to go on the National Institute of Health website and see what I could find about pancreatic cancer. It was as if I were reading about some horrible disease that had struck someone else. How in the world could this be about me? Probably the most shocking thing I read was that only 32% of patients diagnosed with pancreatic cancer are alive one year later. I was sure I would not be one of the lucky ones. I decided, as they say, to put my affairs in order. I decided also that it was time to take that trip to Italy with Julie. I stated looking on line for the right trip. Nothing jumped off the page, and I decided to consult with a travel agency. I knew I wanted to go some time soon. I did a Google search and found a travel agency in San Francisco that specialized in trips to Italy. We put together an itinerary that included Rome, Florence, Milan, and Venice. I knew both of our passports were in order and booked the trip two weeks out. I called Julie and told her we were going.

"Are you crazy?" she said. "Are you insane?"

"No, on the contrary, I am quite sane. This is a trip we've always wanted to take, and there's no time like the present." She knew what I really meant.

"Well, I guess I can find someone to cover the store."

"Close it for two weeks if you have to."

When I got home I showed her the brochure I was given that described our trip.

"Start your vacation in the beautiful in the Italian lake district. Enjoy an included excursion along the shores of its stunning lake and take the ferry to beautiful Bellagio. See Milan's gothic cathedral and romantic Verona on the way to spectacular Venice..."

She hugged me and didn't say a word. We took Emma for a long walk up in the hills above our home.

The next two weeks were busy. I had to prepare for a hearing in Marin Superior Court when we got back regarding Sausalito's desire to close the rehab center that was operating at the old beloved landmark, the Alta Mira. I planned on putting a long list of Sausalito residents on the witness stand testifying how the rehab center was adversely affecting their lives. I knew this would be a stretch, but I knew this was about the only strategy that might work. It depended on how sympathetic the judge might be. We had drawn Judge Wilbur Stuckey, a tree- hugging former hippie who had distinguished himself as a trial lawyer and has been on the bench for seven years. I thought we had a chance of convincing him to take our side. I just didn't know what our argument might be. I set up a lunch the following week with a law school classmate of mine, John Kirkland, who was now teaching at Stanford Law. He was an expert on matters such as Sausalito's problem with the Alta Mira, and I was hopeful he might have some ideas. He was in my study group during my first year in law school at Cal, and we remain fast friends. He had a keen legal mind and wasn't afraid to push boundaries in law. This is exactly what we needed with this case. I never let him forget that be betrayed his alma mater to work for its archrival, Stanford.

Stacey Gordon got her wish, a move to the day shift. The chief appreciated her work on the secret Vincent Check list, albeit without results, and wanted to give her an opportunity to spend more time with her daughter. The problem was this actually gave her the opportunity to spend even more time working. Each evening she poured over the list and continued to try to make some sense out of it with always the same result, nothing was jumping off the page.

Early Tuesday the Police dispatcher got a call from the Alta Mira and sent Stacey to sort things out. An hour before, the handy man at the Alta Mira while making some routine repairs found the two dogs that lived at the Alta Mira dead, their throats slashed. When she arrived she found Alice Perez, the center's administrative assistant, crying.

"How could someone kill two sweet dogs?" she bawled.

"I don't know," Stacey replied wishing there were something more comforting she could say. She asked if they could go inside.

Alice asked her if she wanted coffee. Stacey declined and proceeded to take her statement.

"I know there are a lot of people in Sausalito who don't like us," she said. "But why this? There's a special place in hell for people who do things like this."

Stacey agreed and gave her a hug.

"Have they found who killed Vincent Check?" asked Alice.

Stacey's jaw dropped. "Did you know Mr. Check?" Stacey asked.

"Oh yes, he had been a resident here for a couple months. He was such a nice man. He was always very helpful and willing to do just about anything to help another resident. This is so sad."

"Did you know his family?"

"Not really. He was a trust- fund baby, and money was wired here every month to cover his stay. It came from some bank in Chicago."

"How much does it cost to stay here every month?" asked Stacey.

"Forty thousand dollars"

"You mean that's for someone's entire stay."

"No for each month."

Ten

I couldn't sleep, and got out of bed at about 5 AM. I jumped into the shower and got dressed. I didn't have any clients coming in today so I dressed casually. I put on a pair of khakis and a navy blue sweater. I went quietly into the kitchen and made myself some toast and cereal and sat down at the dining room table and gazed out into the bay. We had been having some remarkably beautiful weather, and today was supposed to be as beautiful as yesterday and the day before. I wondered how people could live in a climate not as perfect as ours. The San Francisco Bay Area is a series of microclimates. Even when it's overcast and cold in most parts of San Francisco, it's typically beautiful in Sausalito.

A few minutes before six I went into the bedroom and gave Julie a peck on the cheek. She opened one eye and smiled. "Where are you going so early?" she asked. "Why don't you come back to sleep for awhile? I guarantee you won't be sorry. I will make you very happy."

" Wow, that's a tempting offer," I smiled. "Can I have a rain Check until tonight?"

"Of course you can. Go ahead and do whatever is so important for you to do, and I'll just go back to sleep."

She was asleep before I got to the door. I looked back and smiled. Even while still in bed first thing in the morning without the benefit of makeup or a brush run through her hair she was still breathtakingly gorgeous. She was sleeping in one of my long sleeve white shirts.

I had an appointment later in the day so I drove to the office, which seemed like a waste of a perfectly nice day for a walk. I left my car with the valet at the Casa Madrona Hotel. Whenever I parked with them I tipped them well, and they always kept my Jag close by. The head valet, Kevin, was already on duty. He told me he was thinking of going to law school and wondered if he could stop by some time. I told him to call me, and I'd buy him lunch. I would do whatever I could to help him. He was a nice kid who always looked after me.

When I got to the office I already had several emails which I disposed of quickly. My morning San Francisco Chronicle was waiting for me. It took me about ten minutes to go through the entire paper. I lamented the fact that we didn't have a better newspaper in San Francisco. I decided that it was time to finally subscribe to the New York Times each morning at the office and made a mental note to call. Sure I could pull it up on the Internet, but there isn't anything quite as satisfying as holding a newspaper in your hands, also not all editorial content made it onto a paper's website.

The phone rang. The caller-ID identified that the call was coming from Jeffrey Summers a local artist and good friend. He wanted to stop by. I told him to come by at 10 AM. There were several things I had to get out of the way including writing a brief that needed to get filed later in the day. Also at 9 o'clock someone was coming in who had a need for my "special" service. I felt so dirty whenever I had a part in ending someone's life. However, I was well aware of the consequences if I didn't fully cooperate.

At precisely none o'clock I heard the door open downstairs and someone make their way up the steep incline to my office. I was surprised to see a young man enter my office.
This wasn't the typical "special client" I had seen in the past. He said his name was Mike, which I knew wasn't the case. He looked extremely nervous, which I guess most people would be if they were making arrangements to end someone's life. He handed me a sealed envelope. I opened it and found in side a cashier's check made out for the proper Amount and payable to the right name.

He explained the would-be victim was his wife, Cindy, whom he has caught cheating on him. He wanted to end her life as soon as possible.

"Isn't this a bit extreme for an act of infidelity?" I asked hoping he might see the error of his thinking and change his mind.

"Not when the person she's sleeping with is my father."

"Ah, I understand." I actually didn't but took the background material he had given me and carefully reviewed it. Cindy was a petite blond who had a come hither look on her face and barely enough clothes on her body to cover the crucial spots.

He looked ready to pass out. I patted him on the back and said, "Don't worry, pal, we'll take care of this right away." For a moment I pondered whether or not I should torpedo this transaction and let the little vixen, Cindy, live. I quickly decided it wasn't worth the risk and sent the information off to the assassin. I didn't know the assassin's real name. "Raven" was all I knew. I didn't know whether or not it was a man or woman. I guess it didn't really matter. Raven was fast and efficient. My stomach turned every time I sent Raven a "deal."

Mike quietly left. I marveled how someone could bring himself to order someone killed no matter what that person had actually done to them. For me this was all in a day's work. I sent the material to Raven through carefully protected email. I locked the check in my drawer and made a mental note to deposit it in the bank the following day.

I then got caught up in a myriad of phone calls, emails, voice mails, and whatever. I glanced at the clock and saw that it was five minutes to ten and knew Jeffrey Summers would soon be walking up the stairs. Moments later the door opened and Jeffrey entered. As usual he was hail and hearty. He slapped me on the back and sat in one of the incredibly uncomfortable chairs in front of my desk. I got up and walked to that side of the desk as well and sat in the facing chair.

"So how have you been?" I asked in a feeble attempt at small talk. He looked very unhappy.

"I'm in trouble," he said. 'I need your help. I don't know where else to turn."

"Sounds serious"

"You have no idea. My life is in shambles."

He seemed extremely agitated and reluctant to talk.

"I can't deal with this right now," he said and got up and left. I was concerned. I had never seen him quite like this before. Nothing ever scared Jeffrey Summers. I almost called him at home that evening but decided not to. If he really needed someone to talk to he'd come running back to me.

Eleven

I was growing exceedingly anxious about my health. Even though my death sentence had been pronounced I was actually feeling rather good. The pain on my right side had more or less subsided. I rationalized that this was the calm before the storm. Julie was an emotional wreck. All she could talk about what how lost she will be after I was gone. I wished there was something I could do to comfort her. I was able to find her a support group for people who had a spouse with a terminal illness. She went a few times and was skeptical about what benefit if any she was getting out of going to the meetings. I counseled her to give it time. I even encouraged her that once she worked through her grief to start seeing someone else. She was too good a woman to spend her life by herself. I even suggested that she go on Match.Com looking for someone. That suggestion didn't go over very well. I also needed someone to talk to. I had no-one. My situation was way too complicated to bring anyone else into the mess.

About four weeks into the program she confessed that it was giving her some degree of comfort going to her group. "I'm really glad," I told her. "Just keep going. It's only a one hour investment of your time each week." She started sleeping better at night and no longer woke up in a cold sweat every night crying.

Last night she came home about an hour later than usual from her meeting. She stopped off with some new friends from the group for coffee. She had called and asked if I minded if she would be home late. To the contrary, I had things on my mind that I needed to think about, some incredibly difficult things. I also welcomed the fact that she would be making some new friends, people she could lean on when I wasn't around any longer. I told her to take her time and enjoy herself. Her whole world could longer revolve around me.

As was my custom, I shut off all the lights and the TV and stared out the window at the boats on the bay and the multi-million dollar homes across the water in Tiburon and Belvedere. Although I had stopped going to mass several years ago I prayed to God to help me make the right decision as to what to do. I was determined to not sit around, watch CNN and just wait to die. I decided as crazy as it sounded I was going to put out a contract on myself.

This was fucking brilliant. I was damned if I was going to sit around and wait to die. Why not put a little adventure into my life and have Raven do the deed. Sure this would be a shock to everyone I knew and be absolutely horrible for Julie, but it would be a lot better than having her come to the hospital every day and wait for me to die so she could get on with her life. I would allow her to get on with her life sooner than later.

I grabbed a legal pad and started writing the things she would need to know. I didn't have to use a phony name. Raven didn't know who I was. Even though I had sent Raven many "assignments" my name was never revealed. It was always more neat and tidy that way. A hit was typically never made right away. Raven carefully studied the person and found the most efficient way to complete the hit. Raven had pulled of the hit on that poor schmuck, Vincent Check, who was found by the concrete elephant in the park across the street from my office. I wondered why Raven had to resort to something as common as a gun shot wound in the temple. Oh well, I wasn't about to question what Raven was doing, he, or was it a she, was very good in their chosen field. I wondered for a moment how someone could kill people for a living and then came to the realization that I wasn't that much better. In many ways I was responsible for these deaths as much as Raven was. Without me as part of the equation there would be nothing for Raven to do. I was enabling Raven to murder. I wondered who would take over for me after I was gone and keep Raven busy.

I grabbed a pad of paper and turned on the reading light that was next to my chair. I started listing the information I would sent Raven. It was the same stuff I would send her on any victim. It seemed strange providing her with a dossier on myself.

Name: Scott Foster Butler
Address: 1713 Bridgeway, Sausalito CA 94965
Occupation: Self-Employed, Attorney
Business Address: 645 Bridgeway, Sausalito CA 94965
Usual Work Day: Leaves home at 7 AM, back home at 6 .PM
Favorite Lunch Spots, Poggio and Paradise Bay, both Sausalito
Wife/Significant Other: Julie Ann Butler
Vehicle: 2002 Jaguar S Class/ Black
License: JULS1965

I was glad I had started the process. I checked to make sure Julie was asleep in the bedroom. She had turned on the ever-present HGTV and had dozed off watching a show about re-doing your kitchen on a budget. She was sound asleep in a pink Ralph Lauren Polo dress shirt that I had given her years ago.

I walked over to the computer and transmitted the information to Raven. I also included several photos that lived on my home computer. I then made sure I deleted this transmission from the "sent" folder. I certainly didn't want Julie finding what I had sent. It was a strange feeling ordering my death. I prayed I had done the right thing. Once a hit is out you can't call it back. I knew my life would never be the same. In a strange way I was looking forward to the adventure that was ahead. Unfortunately, I had no idea what actually be involved.

Twelve

The mind is a complex instrument. It's hard to control what we think. As soon as I had sent Raven the hit on myself I started to become extremely paranoid. Not knowing who the person was that I had just sent the order to kill me I immediately became suspicious of just about everyone around me. Was the assassin local or from somewhere else in the country? The letter carrier that stopped by my office every afternoon started to look at me in a peculiar way. I envisioned the managing director at my favorite restaurant, Poggio, as possibly being Raven. Or could it be the produce clerk at the local Mollie Stone's supermarket? I just started looking at everyone differently. I also suddenly had the feeling that everyone else was now looking at me differently than before. I hadn't anticipated it having this effect on me.

At first it was almost fun, but once I got into the second week it became an ordeal. I knew someone was out looking for a convenient way to have me expire. I didn't know who, and my mind started playing tricks on me. I secretly wondered if Julie could actually be Raven. I decided that plot would have been a little too much like the movie, "Mr. and Mrs. Smith" but quickly convinced myself that was simply too far-fetched and out of the question. I didn't expect to be gunned down on the street any time soon. I knew Raven was looking for an opportune way to kill me.

When I walk by strangers on the street I try to not make eye contact. Don't forget, as a tourist destination Sausalito has many tourists walking the streets each and every day of the year. Sometimes I would walk down to the ferry landing and wait for the next ferry from San Francisco to arrive. I was obsessed, and it became a game wondering who Raven might be. Maybe Raven would be arriving on the ferry. Why not?

For several days I was convinced Raven was the new barista that started work a few weeks ago at Starbuck's. She was a beautiful woman in her mid-20s who always asked me a lot of questions every time I came in. Things like, "So do you work near here?" or "How long have you lived in Sausalito?" or stuff like that. I finally decided that she wasn't an evil assassin but rather a beautiful younger woman flirting with an older guy. I'm not sure whether or not this revelation made me happy or sad. It was the third day in a row that she bought me my morning Carmel latte that made me see what her true intentions actually were.

I suddenly found myself being more jittery than usual. I guess that wasn't too unusual considering the fact that I had just hired someone to kill me. I did take comfort in knowing that in ten days we were due to leave for our trip to Italy. I didn't let Raven know about our trip. Too bad! If she wanted to track me down in Rome or Milan and do the deed there so be it. I didn't believe it was my responsibility to lead her to her prey. I kept wondering when Raven would try to kill me and by what means.

As was the norm, I got to the office early that Wednesday morning. I found myself doing something unusual on the way to work that morning. I would always walk the exact same route, down through the Caledonia Street business district on the same side of the street as Sushi Ran, the great sushi restaurant and right past the movie theater and on to Bridgeway. That morning I walked down Bridgeway took a left at Caffee Trieste and walked along the water till

I was across from my office and crossed Bridgeway, unlocked my door, and headed up the stairs. In some small way I wondered if I was doing something to try to run from Raven. I suddenly felt very clever. But I knew it would be difficult to fool Raven.

When I turned on my computer I found 67 new emails waiting for me. Half of them were meaningless spam that my spam filter neglected to catch. One of the others was an email from Jeffrey Summers, apologizing that he wouldn't be able to make our new appointment. He said that something terrible had happened. I liked Jeffrey and was worried that he might be in trouble. In his email he indicated that he would be out of touch all day and promised to call me the next day. I had a feeling that would not be the case. He was now trying to avoid me.

There was also an email from a woman named Donatella Carpasio. I had no idea who she was. In the later part of the email she used the secret word, "thunder storm" that indicated she was coming to see me at 5.PM to order a hit. Every time I got an email like this I got sick to my stomach. I was tempted this time to refuse to do the task. I was no longer worried about myself. I actually wanted to die, but I was worried about Julie and .what they might do to her. I wasn't about to take any kind of risk at all. Julie still had a full life ahead of her. I fantasized how she would meet someone else after I was gone and settle down into a happy marriage. This was something I wanted for her but could not accept the fact that I would not be the one she would grow old with. It was painful to think of Julie with someone else.

Josh Asher called about an hour after I got to the office to see how I was feeling. I told him not bad at all. I told him about our upcoming trip to Italy. There was suddenly silence on the phone.

"Scott, I know how much this trip means to you," he said. "I want you to have this special time with Julie, but I have moved mountains and have gotten you into very high profile clinical trial. If we have any hope at all of saving you it's going to be with something like this trial."

I didn't know what to say. I knew how much Julie was looking forward to this trip and how much I was looking forward to being with Julie.

"I'm not telling you not to go," he said. "I'm strongly suggesting that you delay it for only 30 days. The beginning of the treatment is crucial. C'mon, Scott, let's make a real heroic try for a happy ending."

I told him I would consult with Julie. I found her ready to lock the door and go to her shop.

"Of course we should delay the trip," she said. "What are you thinking? Maybe you've given up, but I sure haven't. Reschedule the trip. Please. Even if this buys you another few months it's certainly worth it. Scott, call Josh back right now."

By this time I couldn't give a rat's ass whether or not I lived or died, but I didn't want to cause Julie any further mental anguish and told her I would. I called the travel agent that had booked the trip and told her I had a medical emergency and wanted to delay the trip for four weeks. She thought this wouldn't be a problem.

"I give this tour operator a lot of business," she said. "There should be absolutely no problem at all changing the date." I thanked her. She said she should be able to get back to me by the end of the day. I called Josh Asher back and told him what we were going to do. He sounded relieved. I called Julie back as well.

"What were you thinking?" she asked. "Why did you think you had to call me and ask me? Your life and my entire future at stake." She hung up on me which was her normal course of action when she was frustrated with me which seemed to be most of the time. I smiled. It was obvious that Julie was feeling better.

Stacey Gordon was becoming increasingly frustrated with her progress in moving the investigation along. Her usual insider reliable sources had come up with absolutely nothing. She decided to take the game up a notch and actually interview everyone on the list. She decided to not mess around and start with the Mayor, Mike Long. The Mayor in Sausalito was more or less a ceremonial title. The members of the city council would take turns and name one of their own to be Mayor for a one year period of time. It was currently Mike Long's turn "in the barrel." Mike's normal profession was as a real estate developer. She called city hall and got his phone number at his office in San Francisco. His office was in a small red building in a tony section of the city called Pacific Heights. He primarily bought old strip centers, got the proper zoning, and redeveloped these centers into luxury condos. He quickly became a very wealthy man.

She had met him a few times over the past several years and was uncertain whether or not he would remember her name. She thought

Raven

the last time was at a neighborhood watch presentation Stacey had taken part in a few months back in the City Council chambers.

"Of course I know who you are," he said after she called and introduced herself. "Is anything wrong? Why are you calling me?" he sounded concerned. She was surprised by his reaction. He knew damn well why she was calling.

"Nothing to worry about, sir" she said. "I'm working on a very complicated investigation and would like to have an opportunity to ask you some questions."

"What's it about?" he asked sounding more upset by the minute.

"It's a rather complicated situation, and I would rather talk to you about it in person. Do you take the ferry or drive into the city?" she asked.

"I take the ferry, of course. I'm back at 6:10PM."

"Great. I'll meet you when you get off the boat. Have a great day."

She hung up before he could have an opportunity to ask more questions.

When he got of the ferry he saw her leaning against the stone wall on the north side of the ferry landing. He walked over and shook her hand.

"Good to see you again, Mr. Mayor," she said.

"Please call me Mike."

"Okay, Mike. Got time for a cup of coffee?" she asked,

"Yes, I have time, and no, I'm not going to let you buy."

They drove over to the North Star Coffee Company which shared the same parking lot as Paradise Bay. It was the dinner hour, and they were the only customers in the small building.

"What can I get you?" he asked.

"Just get me whatever you're having," she said. "I'll be out back."

North Star Coffee Company occupied a small red building that had housed various businesses over the years including a hair salon, surf shop, and tarot card reader. Nothing was ever considered to be too unusual in Sausalito. Although it was a hot location when it first opened it was now fighting for survival.

Minutes later Mike Long emerged with two large cups of coffee.

"I'm not sure how you take it," he said.

"Black's just fine," she said, pulling a small sheet of paper out of her pocket.

"Ever run into something that just doesn't make sense?" she continued.

"Happens all the time, especially here in Sausalito." She politely laughed.

"You may remember what happened not too long ago. I found a guy killed with a single bullet in the forehead lying by one of the concrete elephants downtown."

"Of course I remember that. How terrible!"

"In his pocket we found a list of names with your name at the top. Any idea what your name was doing in the pocket of a guy who had just been assassinated?

"I had heard about that list. I never met the man and certainly have no idea why my name or the names of the others would be in his pocket."

Stacey was not surprised by this response and handed him a business card.

"If you think of anything please give me a call."

He was hiding something. She could tell he wasn't telling the truth and would have to see how this played out. Truth would prevail. He had carefully thought out what she might ask and what the safest question would be to each question.

Thirteen

Jeffrey Summers was becoming more and more agitated. He had given up trying to sleep at night. He got by with just a couple short naps throughout the day. The mental anguish he was suffering was the result of knowing something that you weren't supposed to know. In his early 60s, Summers was solidly built. At 5'8" and 220 pounds his physical presence made a definite statement that he wasn't someone that you wanted to mess around with. In reality he was a gentle and often misunderstood individual. He tended to be everyone's best friend and confidant. It was hard to not like Jeffrey.

Summers was a talented artist whose technique was called assemblage. He had moved to California from Boston years ago when he finally gave up on winter. Like many artists his talent far surpassed his business acumen. In order to make ends meet he worked several mornings each week as a gardener on the estate of a long-time friend. In another life he owned a company that produced t-shirts for musical acts. Now in his early 60s he was still quite the ladies' man. In a city largely devoid of middle-aged single straight men he found himself quite the popular commodity at dinner parties and wherever single women 50+ might be as guests. He also supplemented his income by supplying several friends with marijuana that he was able to buy from a grower in Petaluma about an hour north of Sausalito.

He suddenly became reclusive but soon figured out staying home wouldn't do much for guaranteeing his safety. Everyone knew where he lived. He briefly entertained the idea of buying a gun but soon realized the thought repulsed him and that he would probably do something stupid like actually shooting himself in the foot. He did own an illegal knife but knew that would do little to protect him. If someone was coming after him he'd probably become too unraveled and not be able to use it.

He found it difficult to go anywhere without being fearful for his safety. One of his favorite weekend rituals was going to the gigantic farmers' market every Saturday at the Ferry Building in San Francisco. He has regular friends he liked to hang out with and looked forward to their company, but he found it hard to drive over the Golden Gate Bridge, ease over to the Embarcadero and drive over to the ornate white historical building that been painstakingly restored eight years prior. When he did go he made sure to take someone else along. He thought it was safer that way. However, he never let his companion know why all of a sudden he was looking for company for a trip where he always flew solo.

That Sunday his date for the morning, a skinny anorexic woman named Rosa backed out at the last minute claiming a migraine. Jeffrey knew the headache was the result of a hangover rather than anything more exotic. Against his better judgment he decided to go into the city by himself. Although he normally drove the high coat of gas, now inching towards $4.00 a gallon, made it more efficient for Jeffrey to take the ferry. It took about a half hour to leave the ferry landing in Sausalito and arrive at the ferry building in San Francisco.

At first Jeffrey decided to sit outside in the front of the boar to enjoy the beautiful weather. Shortly after finding a seat outside he became uncomfortable when two men in dark suits sat down on an adjacent bench and appeared to be gesturing at him and speaking in some language he didn't recognize. He got up and sat down inside the ferry boat Marin, making every effort not to make eye contact with anyone. This feeling of paranoia was an unusual one for him. He knew someone was after him but didn't know who.

Jeffrey briefly dozed off and woke when the captain made an announcement welcoming everyone to San Francisco. For a moment he didn't know where he was but quickly shook off the sleepiness and approached the exit where he would disembark as soon as the ferry was safely docked. While waiting he carefully studied the other passengers. He didn't see the two men who had convinced him to move inside. He wondered where they might be. Everyone else looked fairly normal. When it was finally time to leave the ferry he was the third passenger off. Upon leaving the ferry area he quickly looked for the booth manned by the Fortucci brothers. They sold great organic bell peppers and if you asked them nicely would include some incredibly tasty weed. You had to be flexible and nimble to survive in today's uncertain economy.

"Where have you been?" joked Richie Fortucci feigning concern.

"I've been around. Thanks for being concerned."

"Stay close," said Richie. Some guys have been coming around asking for you."

"Who were they?"

"No idea. They wore expensive Italian suits and blank stares. You know the type!

"Ah, that tells me a lot. Could be just about anyone," he laughed.

"They said they'd stop by later on today to see if you ever showed up. They said they needed to speak with you as soon as possible."

"And what are you going to say if they do?"
"I'll say, "Jeffrey who?""

"You're fucking brilliant."

"Yes, I know."

Fourteen

Julie needed someone to talk to. She was determined to stay strong for Scott and was still going to her weekly support group, which helped but wasn't what she really needed right now. Julie knew a lot of people in Sausalito but had few close friends. Julie and Scott did everything together. There was little time for anyone else. She picked up the phone and called Kate O'Hara, a woman she had met only months ago at political rally for a local candidate. They hit it off really well, and Julie wanted to see if she'd like to meet for lunch. Kate was delighted to hear from her and immediately agreed to meet.

Although Julie would have preferred to meet at Poggio she knew Scott ate there just about every day and didn't want to run into him. Instead she suggested Dario's Pizza and Pasta on Bridgeway near the north side of town. It was a place primarily frequented by locals. That was a good thing. She was in no mood to run into a bunch of tourists. She wanted to go to a place where she could have some serious adult conversation with Kate. Dario's was never busy at lunch, and this would be the perfect place.

Kate O'Hara was originally from Michigan and settled in Sausalito about 22 years ago. Now in her early 50s she looked and acted a lot younger. She had a certain bigger than life flair about her. For a few years she drove around town in a Bentley which everyone knew damn well she didn't own but never-the-less it added a lot to her quirky persona. Not particularly beautiful she was what one might consider cute. She stood about 5' 11" and wore trendy Good Will attire. She too felt connected to Julie since their initial meeting and looked forward to visiting with her over lunch. She wasn't a big fan of Dario's but found nothing wrong with letting Julie choose the place for lunch.

When Julie arrived at Dario's she found Kate already waiting. Kate had the Wall Street Journal open on the table and seemed particularly interested in one story about the next big thing in Silicon Valley. Seeing Julie approach the table she got up, gave Julie and hug, and a peck on each cheek. "Julie, why do you always look so darn cute?" she asked. Julie blushed and joined her at the table. She and Scott had decided to keep his illness a secret for the time being, and Kate would be one of the few people who would learn what was actually going on. She felt guilty by betraying a trust when she told Kate about Scott.

"Kate, thanks for agreeing to meet me for lunch," she said

"Why are you thanking me? It's absolutely my pleasure. It's good to see you, How's Scott?" Julie knew that deep down inside Kate had a crush on Scott.

"I'm hungry," said Julie. "Let's go ahead and order." She was putting off telling Kate about Scott's illness.

They decided to share a medium pepperoni pizza. Julie asked for a Diet Coke. Kate said she'd stick with water.

The two women exchanged pleasantries and talked about everything from the trendy new hair salon in town, Hair Heaven, which was housed in the same building the late much lamented restaurant Christophe's, used to call home to the upcoming Friday night Blues in the Park concert series.

"Kate, I hope you have some time. I need someone to talk to."

"I've got all the time in the world. What's up? Are you okay? Are you and Scott not getting along?"

"Scott's got cancer."

"What? I can't believe what I'm hearing. I saw him in Poggio the other day, and he looked so healthy."

"You heard me right. He's got pancreatic cancer, and the doctor says he may have only a couple months to live. I feel like my life is going up in flames."

"I don't know what to say."

The two sat in silence. Julie started crying. Kate grabbed her hand.

"You know you can't give up," said Kate. "There are all kinds of good things   happening all the time in cancer research. You and Scott have to fight the good fight."

"I know, but it looks like I'm going to lose my Scott. I don't know how I will go on without him. This hasn't yet sunk in "I'm trying to stay really strong for him, and it's not easy."

"Maybe you don't need to. It's okay to let him know how afraid you are."

"I can't let him see me falling apart. I don't want him to feel guilty for getting sick."

"It's okay to cry around Scott."

"Can't do it. I just can't do it."

"Are you getting help with this?"

"I'm in a support group

"It's better than nothing I guess."

"I'm going to ask my friend Evan who's a therapist if he can refer you to someone who works in this delicate area."

"Thank you." She put her head in her hands and didn't say a word for almost a half hour."

"So what else can I do for you?" asked Kate.

"Nothing. Just being here with me has meant a lot."

"You know my phone numbers. I know things will be getting really difficult for you. Please don't hesitate to call me at any time."

"If you see Scott please don't tell him that you know. He wants to keep this private as long as possible."

"I promise."

They finished their lunch and agreed to get together for breakfast the following week. Julie was happy that she had the wisdom to reach out to Kate and knew how much she would need her friendship in the months ahead. It was hard going through this without a vast network of friends.

Fifteen

"The night was cold. The moon was yellow, and the rain came tumbling down."

The sounds of the Lloyd Price oldie,"Stagger Lee"came blaring through Scott's I-Pod as he and Emma walked down Bridgeway toward downtown Sausalito. Scott had a terrible day and needed some time with Emma to try to bring him back to some sense of normalcy, whatever that meant. Emma was a sympathetic listener. Julie was in a snarky mood, and this was the perfect time for a long overdue walk. He purposely left his cell phone at home. He needed some quiet time.

He had gotten a visit that day from a man who simply described himself as Frank. The man came to Scott's office near the end of the day seeming very upset. He was a short man dressed in a brown suit that looked like it had just come off the rack at Goodwill .He was close to five foot two and looked like he had led a long and confused life. The man told him that it was his understanding Scott could take care of delicate little problems. Scott told him that it all depended on what the problem might be.

"There's a fella I want to send to his just reward." said Frank.

"What?"

"You heard me. There's an artist in Sausalito that I want to meet a painful death."

"Tell me more."

"His name is Jeffrey Summers. I want him dead."

Of course, knew Summers well. I didn't reveal that to the man. I collected in cash $40,000 and helped the man fill out the questionnaire about the intended victim.

"I believe he has lunch at Paradise Bay most days."

I knew that was the case since many days he was the one Summers was having lunch with. I thanked the man for his business and said they would let him know when the task had been accomplished. The man left. I at down at my desk and stared out the window. What in the world could I do? Summers was a close friend. What if the bad guys sent this guy in as a test? If I didn't set the assassination in place would they kill me and Julie? There was no easy answer. This is what I had been dreading- the order to kill someone I knew and cared about. There was no way I was going to arrange the death of Jeffrey Summers. I would find a way to sidetrack this request.

Scott and Emma made it to downtown Sausalito and walked right by the doorway to his small office. He was tempted to go up and clear his email but decided that could wait till the next day. He paused for a moment. Emma wanted to keep walking and took off towards home. He decided he had enough alone time and accommodated Emma's wishes.

The sun was setting over San Francisco Bay. The sky was a bright orange over the Golden Gate Bridge. This reminded Scott why he was so fortunate to live there. If life wasn't so complicated this would be the best time of his life. He married the girl of his dreams, and although they didn't have any children they still had a full life. He wondered how much longer it would last. He wondered if he had done the right thing, ordering his own death. He wondered what Raven was doing with "the order." Was this something that Raven was planning on taking care of soon, or were there other "orders" ahead of him? Did Raven work with other conduits such as Scott or was Raven there primarily there just for Scott? These were some things he probably would never know. He started to hope that he wasn't a priority so he'd have more time with Julie. Every day became more and more precious. He wanted to make the most of the time he had left.

* * *

Sixteen

It was 8 AM Saturday morning. I got up early to cook breakfast for Julie and myself. I used to worry about my cholesterol and would have never made scrambled eggs and bacon in the past, but I decided it was silly to worry about that any more. I went to Safeway in Mill Valley the night before and bought a dozen eggs, Jimmy Dean bacon, and orange juice for the morning meal. I enjoyed preparing a meal for the two of us. It was something nice I could do for Julie, and she always really appreciated it. I had started doing this for years ago. I went outback, picked some flowers and put them in a vase on the table.

It was a beautiful morning, and several sailboats were already heading out from Sausalito for a day on San Francisco Bay. I enjoy sailing and from time to time entertained the idea of taking lessons but knew that would have only led to me wanting to buy my own boat, which was something I could ill afford to do. Several friends owned boats, and Julie and I were invited out six or eight times each year. Most of the time it was a bit too cold for anyone but the hard - core sailor to go out on the Bay. The warm months in San Francisco were September and October. It rarely gets into the 70s during the summer and quite often it's really windy. Only the hardiest sailors sail all year long.

I had wanted for some time to sit down with Julie and help her plan what life would be without me. There was no easy way to do this kind of thing. I had spent the last couple weeks getting our financial situation in order. Julie wouldn't have to work unless she really wanted to. I wanted her to know where all of our limited investments were and what debts would still be out there, which were minimal, that she would have to take care of after I was gone. I had prepared a folder for Julie that included statements from all of our accounts and the phone numbers of our attorney, CPA, and other key advisors. Yes, even attorneys have an attorney, accountant, and a financial advisor. I had already spoken with each one of them, told them about my illness, and asked them to please take care of Julie after I was gone. Needless to say I said nothing regarding the way I was actually expecting to die. I told them about the cancer and nothing else.

Julie rolled out of bed about 8:20 in her PJs with little rubber ducks on them, ran a brush through her hair, walked over to the table where I was sitting and gave me a kiss on the cheek.

"Good morning," she whispered. I just smiled. "What's for breakfast?" she asked.

I handed her the morning paper and told her I'd be right back. I brought out the eggs, bacon, fresh fruit, and toast.

"Wow, I'm impressed," she smiled.

"And you should be." I said returning the smile. Even though the subject matter would not be pleasant, I didn't want breakfast to turn into a maudlin affair.

We enjoyed our meal and exchanged small talk about friends.

"I can't imagine what life is going to be like without you," she said softly.

"Oh you'll be just fine," I said holding back tears. "You're strong, resourceful and…"

She came over and sat down on my lap. "Hold me," she said.

We sat there for over an hour. She wept softly. I didn't know what to say so said nothing. It was now after ten.

"After I'm gone," I said, not believing the words that were coming out of my mouth, "I want to make sure that things are as smooth as possible for you financially."

I handed the folder to Julie and said. "I was going to go over everything in this folder in great detail, but I won't. It's all pretty self-explanatory. Take a peek and let me know if you have any questions."

She gave me a hug and said, "Let's go for a walk."

Emma crawled out from under the table. I grabbed her leash. Julie went to her closet to get a sweater.

"You're going out in your ducky jammies?" I asked.

"Why not, Scott? Why not?"

Exactly, why not!

Seventeen

Stacey Gordon got off her shift at 5.PM, and thanked her lucky stars that she was now working the day shift. She went home to the small house she shared with her daughter, Natasha, and their dog, Scooter. The dog was a gentle but incredibly ugly dog that looked like the love child of basset hound and lab. They had adopted Scooter from the Marin Humane Society, and Natasha and Scooter slept together each night.

As Stacey walked in the door Natasha rushed over to give her a hug and showed her a picture of the Golden Gate Bridge that she had colored in school that day. She was so proud.

"That's absolutely beautiful," Stacey gushed. "We're going to hang it right here and now on the fridge. Go get me the tape."

Stacey found an empty space on the top of the refrigerator door and hung the picture.

"Perfect," she said. "It makes the whole room look better."

Natasha proudly beamed. She loved pleasing her Mom. She still missed her Dad even though for quite awhile he hadn't been around much. Most weeks she got to see him for a couple hours on Sunday afternoon. Stacey was just fine with that. She wanted Natasha to have a relationship with her Dad.

Stacey exchanged pleasantries with her sister who was also enjoying the fact that Stacey was now on the day shift. They hugged, and she walked her sister to the front door. They discussed spending a day shopping together on Stacey's next day off. They hadn't had a girl's day out in a long time. Stacey promised to plan the whole day and let her sister know all the details.

"So what do you have a taste for tonight?" Stacey asked Natasha, already knowing the answer.

"Pizza!"

"I knew it!" smiled Stacey. "Pepperoni, right? Thin crust?"

"Yup."

"Okay, you've got it.' She picked up the phone and called Dario's and was told the pizza would be there in about a half hour. "How are you doing on your homework?" she asked Natasha.

"Almost done," she answered.

"Okay, go finish it, and let me take a peek when you're done."

Natasha returned to her bedroom. Stacey looked at the mail. Nothing too exciting was waiting. She opened the utility bill from PG&E and was pleased to see it was only $22.81. Stacey went to the refrigerator and pulled out an already open bottle of Chardonnay and poured herself a glass. At one time she thought she was drinking too much and now treated herself to a single glass of wine when she got home each night.

She walked to her bedroom and looked in the mirror. Stacey just turned 38 and thought she looked really good for her age. She was tall, thin, and looked like someone who might have played sports in college. She actually attended San Francisco Community College for two years and was too busy with a full time job to play sports. She had short brunette hair and from time to time had thought of growing it out but figured short hair was better on a cop. Men found her attractive. She wished she had more time to do girly things like going for a facial or buying and applying the right kind of makeup. She had adapted well to the challenges of being a single mom but didn't necessarily have to like it. Although she was crazy busy during the day and loved being with Natasha she was still lonely.

Her recent meeting with Mike Long had been very frustrating. He claimed absolutely no knowledge of how his name wound up in the pocket of a dead man, and not just any dead man, but a dead man who was an active member of the Chicago mob. How in the world could this be the case? She was sure that by now everyone on the list knew about her meeting with Long. However, she needed to press on. Tomorrow she would call the others on the list and arrange meetings. She was interested to see if all of their stories would be the same. She would soon know.

She was especially interested in Sid Emmett and would call him first. Emmett started the local newspaper, the. Marin Times, 35 years ago, and sold it several years ago to a multimillionaire who had moved to Sausalito from India. The new owner then hired Emmett to run the paper. This was the kind of sweetheart deal that everyone dreamed of. He got his cake and was enjoying eating it day after day.

Sid Emmett was in his late 60s, wore his hair in a pony tail, and looked like he was hopelessly stuck in the 1960s. He considered himself to be quite the man around town. He wasn't as important as he thought himself to be. He has his small group of friends, but in recent years people started avoiding him. However, his name was on the list with others that was found in the late Vincent Check's pocket. It didn't get there by accident.

She picked up the telephone and called Sid Emmett's home phone number. Voice mail answered after the fifth ring. She wasn't surprised. "Mr. Emmett," she said. This is Officer Gordon with the Sausalito Police; I'm working on a case that you may have some information on. Please call me. I work the day shift. Thanks," She added her phone number to the message and hung up.

She wondered whether or not she'd hear back from him. She'd keep trying. She then started calling others on the list. She wasn't as far along as she wanted to be and was determined to meet with everyone on the list before the end of the week.

Natasha bounced back into the room. "Homework's all done, Mommy," she proclaimed.

"Goodness gracious, you're quick," said Stacey. "Let me see." Natasha proudly showed her the math work sheet she had just completed. It was the 3 and 4 multiplication tables. Stacey checked all the work and reported back that everything was perfect.

"Nice job, Natasha!" Natasha was a very bright precocious little girl. Stacey was proud. She thought that someday she may meet someone special and remarry and possibly have another child, but if she didn't she knew she hit the jackpot with Natasha.

The doorbell rang. It was the pizza. Scooter barked. Natasha grabbed him by the collar and yanked him into the kitchen.

Stacey grabbed her purse and gave the delivery guy a $20 bill, and told him to keep the change.

"C'mon sit down," said Stacey to her daughter. "Let's have some girl talk. I'm off duty for the night."

This was her favorite part of the day.

Eighteen

I got to the office about 9 AM. Yeah, it was a little later than usual, but Julie was putting in a large order for needlepoint and needed some help figuring out what she actually needed. In reality I think she was just looking for an excuse to have me hang around the house a bit longer. That was just fine with me. I thought I might start hanging around the needlepoint shop more just to spend more time with her not knowing how much time I actually had left. This was one of those bittersweet mornings.

My paranoia has reached a new level. It's gotten to the point where I have stopped looking people in the eye when I walk down the street. I have stopped going to Starbuck's in the morning. The new barista there is just asking too many questions. I keep my door locked during the day. The letter carrier is now putting my mail through the slot in the door. I have canceled my cleaning service. You never know who these people might really be. I figured I could clean my office on my own.

I was starting to have my regrets that I ordered my own demise, but knew there was nothing I could do about it. Once a hit is out it can't be called back. That's just the way it was done. "All sales are final." But in my heart of hearts I knew I had done the right thing. At the end of the day it would be easier on Julie.

I checked my email. Nothing there too exciting. Somehow I was expecting to have an email from Raven. I don't know why, but I really wanted to know more about this mysterious person. Was it a man or woman? What kind of work did he or she do as a cover? What did they look like? I thought with the name "Raven" the person probably had dark hair, but who in the world could tell. My mind was drifting. I would hope I would know who Raven was before I was dead.

There was yet another hearing coming up the next day regarding the Alta Mira law suit in Superior Court in San Rafael. I spent the morning getting ready for the hearing. I was rarely stumped regarding strategy in case, but time I wasn't sure what a winning strategy might be. The Alta Mira had hired an attorney named SAM Singer to represent their interests. Singer was a partner in a large San Francisco law firm. They were hauling out the heavy fire power, and I knew I had to be at the top of my game. It was hard concentrating having so many other things on my mind. I knew I would have to rise to the occasion or Singer would squash me like a bug. He was an absolute viper and would do whatever it took to finish off an opponent and typically fought dirty.

The telephone was mercifully quiet that morning. The one call I did get was from someone looking to put a hit out on someone. Every time I got a call like this I got an upset stomach. I went over the parameters of what I needed and agreed to meet with this person in two days. I had installed a dedicated line for this dark side of my business. The number was given to prospective clients when they made an initial inquiry.

.

As usual I locked up the office around noon and walked over to Poggio for lunch. I felt safe there and decided to linger over lunch for a couple hours. I brought along my newspapers and was determined to settle in for the long run. My Grey Goose martini arrived within minutes of me taking my seat. Amy, the Managing director of Poggio, came over to my table, removed the "Reserved" sign, and gave me a peck on the cheek. She smiled and didn't say a word.

I opened the "Wall Street Journal" and started to read page two. I was having a hard time concentrating. For a moment I wondered whether or not someone might try to poison my food as a quick and easy to do me in. "That's rubbish," I said to myself. "How stupid is this. I know the people in the kitchen. Why would they…" I grumbled in disgust with my foolish thoughts and slammed down my martini. Moments later my second one arrived. .I didn't even have to ask. This is why I came here every day. In a strange way I envied others who were chosen to meet their maker. They didn't have to endure the paranoia that was now almost totally engulfing me.

There was a mixture of both tourists and locals in the restaurant. Several people came over to say hello. I briefly wondered if one of them might be Raven but decided to stop this foolish thinking. The mind can do terrible things if you let it. When Raven was ready to kill me, there was probably not a lot I could do to prevent it.

I ordered the snapper like I did most days and bemoaned the fact that I had gotten so predictable and quickly went back to my newspaper. The second martini did the trick. I decided to allow myself just one more. I was in a safe place and was in no hurry to leave.

I took the elevator up to the men's room, which was actually on the second floor of the hotel itself. I splashed some cold water on my face, trying to calm myself down. I was having a panic attack, which was happening more and more frequently. I wondered if Josh Asher could give me something to help work through these attacks.

On the way back to my table I stopped by a table near the door where Howe Steiner was sitting. He would be coming with me to the Alta Mira hearing the following day. I told him to meet me outside my office at 8 AM.

My third martini was waiting when I returned. I swore this would be my last. Strangely enough I didn't feel anything from the two I already consumed. Moments later my snapper arrived accompanied by wild rice and green beans. I convinced myself they were safe and took my first bite. It was delicious, and I consumed it faster than usual. I briefly considered splurging and getting dessert and decided against it.

I got back to my office shortly before 2:30 and called Julie.

"What's up?" she asked.

"Not a damn thing. I just called to tell you how much I love you."

"Aw. That's nice. You've got to do this more often."

Suddenly I got very serious. "I'm sorry I haven't done more little things like this in the past. Please forgive me."

"What's gotten into you? It's okay, Scott. It's okay."

Nineteen

Mike Long reached over and grabbed his cordless phone that was sitting on the opposite side of the couch. He was all-consumed with watching the Giants getting pummeled by the Braves. For a moment he couldn't remember where he had put it but found it under a pillow.

Sid Emmett was on the other end. "What the fuck is going on, Mike?"

"You sound upset, Sid. What's wrong?" He knew damn well what was wrong.

"This chick, Stacey Gordon, from the Police has been calling wanting to meet."

"So?"

"What do you mean?"

"She wants to talk about Vincent Check and why all of our names were on a piece of paper in his pocket."

"Fuck."

"Just be a good boy and meet with her. Just keep your mouth shut and don't tell her a damn thing."

"Do you want me to lie?"

"Just tell here her you don't know a thing about all this. C'mon, Sid, you're a big boy. You should know how to act in a situation like this. Why are you bothering me? The Giants game is on."

"This is crazy."

"Sid, the whole thing is crazy. I suppose I should call the others and tell them to expect a call if they haven't already. Officer Gordon needs to back off this or…"

"Or what?" Sid interrupted.

"Good bye, Sid," he replied and hung up on him.

Mike long picked up the phone and started calling the others one by one.

"Haven't heard a thing," Jim Squires reported.

"Try to avoid her as long as you can, and then don't tell her a thing. Tell her you don't know what's going on. "

He had a similar conversation with the others on the list. No-one else had yet heard from Stacey Gordon, but he knew they would. He cursed the day that he had met Vincent Check. He needed some help on a special project and thought Check could help. He was wrong. Vincent Check turned out to be a low-life hood. Although it was against his nature to wish ill on anyone, he was glad Vincent Check was dead, although he had nothing to do with the actual death.

Mike Long's wife had gone out to run a few errands. It was early evening, and they had not yet had dinner. He decided to make his famous chili which he knew his wife Andrea enjoyed. He was hopeful that he had all the ingredients. He went to the kitchen cupboard and started pulling out what he needed one item at a time. He then went to the freezer and pulled out a one and a half pound of ground beef. All he was missing was a can of tomato paste. He figured he could substitute ketchup and no-one would ever know the difference. He was hungry and hoped she would hurry home.

He carefully chopped the onion and green pepper, set them aside, and started browning the ground beef in a large deep skillet on the stove. When the beef was brown he started blending in the other ingredients. He turned the stove down to low and set the timer. He would let the chili simmer on low for an hour and then it would be ready.

Mike Long was one of the most popular people in Sausalito. He and Andrea moved to the Bay Area fifteen years ago and there was never any looking back. They had tired of the fierce Iowa winters and moved to the Promised Land to seek fame and fortune. To date they had achieved both. They had a good life in Sausalito with plenty of people who cared about them.

Andrea Long was President of the Sausalito Women's Club, an organization that was harder to gain admittance into than San Francisco's famed Town and Country Club. She ran the club with a firm hand and a big smile. People liked Andrea Long and many younger women wanted to be just like her. Now in her early 50s she was still a head turner. She was tall, thin and resembled actress Ali McGraw. She was in her element running the women's club and just won a nearly unanimous vote for a second term.

She returned home and smelled the wonderful spices in the chili filling the room. She walked into the living room. Mike stood. They embraced, She thanked him for preparing dinner and then retreated to her home office to Check her email and return phone calls, one of which was from Julie Butler, wondering how she might become a member of the Sausalito Women's Club. They agreed they would meet the following week for lunch. Julie was looking for a way to sustain herself after Scott was gone. She didn't have a large network of friends since she and Scott did almost everything together. They would rather be with each other than out and about with pals. She thought she'd fit in well with the Sausalito Women's Club and quietly smiled that she was glad she was slowly preparing for life after Scott. This was sad but true. She had to start thinking about how she would take care of herself. She would have to develop a whole new infrastructure for her life.

When they got off the phone Andrea called a few board members and asked whether or not anyone had heard of Julie. No-one knew much about her but they were all familiar with her needlepoint shop.

"I hear she's a really nice person," said one board member. "She's attractive, poised and would probably be a fine new member."

They agreed they would invite her to a meeting so she could be interviewed by the membership at large and see if she passed scrutiny for admittance to this exclusive group of women. They liked the idea that Julie owned her own business and was a successful entrepreneur. They were trying to change the profile of the group from a bunch of socialites to a collection of successful women. Now all they had to do was fine a core group of successful women.

Twenty

It was early afternoon, and I had just gotten back from court. It was yet another hearing in the on-going Alta Mira saga. Howie Steiner, Sausalito council member accompanied me. The Alta Mira legal team was able to get another continuance. It's become an on-going circle jerk. Howie and I stopped off for lunch after the hearing at the San Jose Tauqueria, a seedy little joint which sits under a bridge in San Rafael. They serve the best Mexican food in the Bay Area. My first time there I was taken aback by the stark interior and picnic tables covered with red and white oil cloth, but one time was all it took. I was seduced and prepared to go back there any time the situation presented itself. I noticed that a few people had even brought their dogs into the restaurant, a practice against health department rules but never-the-less gladly tolerated by the restaurant. To say the least it was a very authentic Mexican restaurant.

I was just biting into my carne asada and Howie into his beef enchiladas when my phone rang. I recognized the phone number as being Josh Asher's office as it flashed on the caller ID.

"Hello, this is Scott."

"Scott, this is Rosa. Josh was wondering if you could come by this afternoon."

"Is anything wrong?" I asked.

"I don't know a thing." She answered. "I'm just the messenger."

"How about three thirty?" I asked.

"We'll see you then."

"Everything okay." asked Howie.
"I think so." I had just had some blood work done a couple days ago. I wondered if there was more bad news. Why in the world did he want to see me? It would be a long few hours until I got to see Josh.

We finished our lunch. I barely said a word. Howie sensed there was something on my mind and gave me my space. I appreciated that. I stared out into thin air occasionally apologizing for being lost in my thoughts.

I dropped Howie back at City Hall and thanked him for going with me. It was important to show that someone from the city was interested enough to show up.

"We'll talk soon," I said. Howie waved as he left the car.

I debated whether or not to take Julie with me or even tell her I was going. I elected to neither tell her nor take her. I had a feeling there was bad news ahead and decided to take it like a man and not subject Julie to another visit to UCSF Medical Center.

I headed over the Golden Gate Bridge, turned down 19th Street and made the loop to the right on California Street in order to wind up on the left side of 19th on Clement Street heading toward Geary and then a right on Stanyan to get up to Parnasus where the UCSF campus sits. I was pleased to find a parking place in the 350 Parnasus building on the second level. I though getting there in late afternoon was the secret rather than getting there early in the morning when it typically took over a half hour to find a precious place to leave your car. I headed up the elevator to the first floor and entered Josh's Office, the Executive Health Service.

Rosa was sitting at the front desk. "Have a seat, Scott. Josh will be here in a few minutes. He's on his way over from a meeting in another building. He knows you're coming."

I thanked her and grabbed a seven month old copy of "Time" but found it difficult to concentrate. What in the world did he want to see me about?

About ten minutes later Josh entered. He had a big smile on his face.

"Josh, c'mon in," he said. I wondered if he was going to grant me another three or four months. I was willing to bargain for just about anything. It was strange that he was calling me in. I was feeling really good.

"Scott, I don't know how to tell you this so I just will." I wondered what in the world he was talking about. "I have some incredibly good news for you. There was a massive mix-up. The test results we got back weren't yours." A terrible mistake has been made.

"What are you telling me?"

"I'm telling you that you're healthy. I'm also apologizing to you for the angst we've put you and your family through. No-one here can ever remember this happening before. Aren't you happy? We now have the task of telling the news to the person who thought his tests came back just fine."

I didn't know what to say. "Of course I'm happy. I'm thrilled. I'm not going to tell Julie until I get home. Oh my God!"

"Go home and get your life back on track. I hope I don't see you for a long time. Live long and be happy."

This was an out-of-body situation. I had a hard time thinking straight. I wasn't dying. I wouldn't be leaving my beloved Julie. Oh My!!!

The good news was tempered by a harsh reality. I had put a hit out on myself. Once you put a hit out on someone it can't be recalled. There were no ifs buts or ands about this situation. That was just the way it was. It would be ironic if Raven tried to get to me tonight. There had to be a way to call back Raven. I certainly didn't want to die. The first thing I would do is email Raven and tell her a horrible mistake had been made. I knew she'd probably just laugh. Never the less I had to try. Of course I didn't care about getting back the payment I had made to kill me. I thought of contacting the guys who set me up in this terrible ruse but knew that would not bear fruit.

I didn't want to die. I couldn't let this happen. The hit had been out for some time, and I sensed something might be imminent. Raven was probably lurking someplace nearby ready to do the deed. I decided to call Julie to pack a bag, and I'd be home shortly to drive up to the Wine Country for a celebration.

"What are we celebrating?" she asked.

"I'll tell you tonight. I wanted to add some excitement to the situation."

She was waiting by the door when I got there, bag packed and ready to go. She had gotten our neighbor, Nick, to watch Emma while we were gone. She gave me an embrace and the longest kiss I had gotten in memory.

"So are you going to tell me?" she asked.

"Tell you what?" I said playfully.

"Why are we going away? Why we are celebrating? I love surprises."

"You'll have to wait just a little bit longer," I smiled.

I carried the bag to the car and we set out on our jaunt. We headed north on Bridgeway which fed directly into Highway 101 north. It was past rush hour and was smooth sailing until our turnoff in Novato for Napa. We cranked up the radio, something by The Dave Mathews Band was on and we held hands as we headed east.

We arrived at the Sonoma Mission Inn less than a half hour later. Julie remained in the car while I checked us in. I returned moments later and we drove to the entrance closest to our room. We walked in the entrance, took a left and found room 478. They had upgraded us to a junior suite. I picked up the phone and ordered some brie and champagne from room service.

Julie unpacked our bag and asked, 'what in the world are you up to?''

"Julie, I have some incredible news."

"I'm not dying. I'm just fine."

"What? What are you saying?"

"You heard me. I am not dying. We have many years left together. There was a big mix-up. Those weren't my tests."

"Oh my God!" she started crying; only this time these were joyful tears.

We held each other. We made love, and fell asleep in each other's arms. I woke at 7 AM the next morning. The sun was shining and a major problem was still at hand. I had to somehow call off Raven. I knew this would be next to impossible. I certainly didn't want to die.

I let Julie sleep. I showered and plotted my next move in which now would be an elaborate cat and mouse game with Raven. I had to prevail. This was truly a matter of life or death.

Raven pulled a file off the desk, opened it and read everything Raven needed to know about the next victim.

The name "Scott Butler" was at the top of the page.

"Hmm, Sausalito, that makes it convenient," Raven proclaimed. "It's time to start working on this one."

Twenty-One

Stacey Gordon had one of those days ahead of her that both made her wonder and realize why she chose law enforcement as her career. Her shift wasn't due to start till 9 AM, but she got to the station about an hour early. She stopped at the 7-11and picked up her coffee on the way in. It was a whole lot more pleasant getting coffee at the beginning of her shift than at the end when she was struggling to stay awake. For some strange reason she missed not seeing Azfar each day. She told the young man behind the counter who was diligently putting on the morning's supply of nachos to leave word for Azfar that she said hello. For a moment she wondered whether that would be sending the wrong message but decided to say hello any way. It was already a warm morning and for a brief moment she had pondered getting a Coke Slurpee to get her caffeine but stayed with the coffee. She swore that sooner or later she would break her nasty habit of drinking so much coffee but realized with everything she was going through that this was not the right time to drop her morning Cup of Joe.

The first item on her agenda was a meeting with Special Agent John Toland of the San Francisco office of the FBI. She felt bad that she was not farther along on the investigation.

"Don't worry about a thing," said Toland sitting across the table from her in a small conference room. "However, we do need to move this along. I am a bit concerned that we're not farther along than we are right now. Do you think I should pair you up with one of our people to make sure we are making some progress?"

She had dreaded having this conversation. It was not unexpected. "Give me two weeks. If I have not delivered the goods by that time I will welcome any and all assistance.' This was a lie. She was upset that the FBI felt she couldn't handle it. Sure, she probably should have been a lot farther along than she was right now, but she was determined to turn up the heat.

"Ok, Officer Gordon. I can live with that, but remember it's not a sign of weakness to ask for help." He said sternly. She knew he was losing his patience.

She took him through her plan for the week, answered a few questions, and walked him to the door. She told him to have a good day actually being glad he was gone.

Barry Peterson walked through the door, late as usual. "Is Toland gone?" he asked

.

"You just missed him." She was glad the two didn't connect. She certainly didn't need Toland casting any doubts on her ability with Peterson. She had fought hard to gain his respect and didn't need a setback. Stacey wanted Peterson's support. Success in this investigation might be all it takes.

Stacey grabbed her service revolver out of the safe n the front of the building. It's normal for Police to check their weapons at the door to avoid being compromised by any visitors. She went to her Police cruiser, pulled out the parking lot, and made a right on Bridgeway and headed towards the Shell gas station and car wash on the north side of town. She filled up her car and then ran the car through the car wash. She hadn't washed the car in over a week, and it looked like she had taken her cruiser off-roading. She tipped the young Hispanic woman three dollars who dried off the car. This time she headed south towards the Alta Mira. She wanted to learn more about the stay of Vincent Check in this beautiful compound in the hills of Sausalito over-looking San Francisco Bay. Her first visit there just scratched the surface.

She went through the gate of the Alta Mira and parked her cruiser under a tall shady tree. She walked over to the main building and was greeted at the front door by a tired looking woman named Eleanor who seemed to see a Police officer at the front door and asked, "Is anything wrong officer?"

"No, who's in charge here? I have a few questions."

"That would be our Director, Helen Foster."

"I don't know. I will go see." Stacey knew that Eleanor knew damn well Helen foster was around and that I was there to inquire about the late Vincent Check.

Several minutes later a mousy looking woman resembling Betty Ford approached me and extended her hand. "My name is Helen Foster. I run the Alta Mira. How may I help you?"

"I am here to talk about Vincent Check."

"Of course. What a sad case. He was such a nice young man."

Stacey couldn't believe she was referring to this dead hood as a "nice young man."

"I'd like to reconstruct his stay here. I'm hoping that you will be able to help me."

"I will do what I can."

"Splendid. Is there a place we could go sit and talk, where I can take notes?"

Helen Foster led Stacey up a spectacular spiral staircase to the second floor which had once been the restaurant. She told Stacey to have a seat at a small round table, the kind of table set up for banquets.

"I understand the Sunday brunches here used to be spectacular."

"That's what I hear. Unfortunately I never had the chance to indulge. I was hired and moved her from LA shortly before we were licensed and open for business.

"Would you please tell me how long Vincent Check was a resident here before his death?"

"Mr. Check moved in about a month after we opened. I really shouldn't be telling you much about him with all the privacy laws."

"Confidentiality ceases with the death of a person."
"Are you sure?"

Stacey explained that she was quite sure.

Helen Foster explained that "Vincent Check called to inquire about the rehab programs about two weeks after we opened. He said that his problem was with alcohol. I explained our fees, which run $40,000 per month. He said that was okay. He was motivated to get better and money was no problem. I explained that he should be prepared to be with us for at least six months. He understood. Three days later I had a cashier's Check for his first months stay drawn on the Harris Bank of Chicago."

"So did he arrive on time?"

"He was so motivated that he got here two day's early. He said he wanted the extra time to make himself comfortable in his cottage and to get to know Sausalito. Our residents are only allowed out for a few hours on Sunday afternoons. I guess he just wanted to check things out."

Foster went on to explain that a Check arrived like clockwork every month to pay the fees for Vincent Check's stay.

"How was he as a resident? Did he do what he was supposed to do?"

"Oh he was an absolute joy. He made it to all of his therapy sessions and regularly ate his meals in the restaurant with other residents. At times he seemed a bit distant, but I thought he might just be shy. There was one unusual thing about him. We would always find him lurking in strange places for no reason at all like the sub basement to the main house or in the utility building outback. We never pressed the issue but always thought it was a bit odd. When we emptied out his cottage we did find a number of tools and pieces of sheet rock. Here's a guy who wore expensive suits, had perfectly manicured nails, and looked like he had never picked up a tool in his life.

Stacey thanked Helen Foster for her time and handed her a business card. "Please call me if you think of anything else,"

She left frustrated that she didn't find out anything further realizing that she indeed knew only part of the story. Somehow the Alta Mira itself was a key player in the whole scenario; however she had no idea how.

Raven stared at Scott Butler's photo. "Such a handsome young man. What a pity he's going to die."

Twenty-Two

Sid Emmett looked in his closet. He was due to meet with Stacey Gordon that afternoon and was wondering what he should wear. Was a suit too much? Probably. It would make him look like he was trying to impress her. He decided on a cashmere sweater and grey slacks. He was nervous and hated cops. He used to pal around with Barry Peterson who figured out what a fraud Emmett was and wanted nothing to do with him.

He agreed to meet with Stacey Gordon at the Starbuck's on Princess Street. He got there early, ordered a vanilla latte and waited for her. Stacey arrived about 15 minutes later and bought a small coffee.

She greeted Sid and sat across the table.

Sid tried to stay calm but was sweating profusely.

"Are you okay?" she asked.

"I'm just fine," he said tersely. "Now what can I do for you?"

"Well, Mr. Emmett, I'm sure you know why I wanted to visit. I know you remember the body found recently by one of the concrete elephants in the park."

"I do."

"Well what confuses me is that fact that your name and phone number was found on a piece of paper in his suit pocket. Do you have any idea what this man with ties to organized crime was doing with your name and phone number in his pocket? Help me understand all this. It doesn't make sense."

Sid explained that he had heard about this list but had no idea why his name was in Vincent Check's pocket. "I never had the pleasure of meeting Mr. Check. I share your confusion."

"Oh come one," she smiled. "A man with ties to organized crime is found with a bullet in his head lying in the park. Your name is in his pocket. I'm not the smartest gal in the world but something's wrong with this picture. C'mon, Mr. Emmett, help me out."

He knew she thought he was full of shit and became more uncomfortable.

"Don't know a thing," he insisted. "And if you'll excuse me I've got to get to work."

She thanked him not surprised with his lack of response. It s obvious that he knew something, possibly the entire story. She now had to find out what he knew and what his involvement was. He would be a hard person to crack. She knew sooner than later she could get him to talk.

Twenty-Three

I normally like a challenge but have never ever been faced with something quite like this. Someone has been hired to take my life. The person who hired the assassin to kill me was actually me. Once a hit is out it can't be taken back. I elected to not tell Julie yet about this bizarre situation I found myself in. I wasn't sure what, if anything, I could do about it.

We stayed at the Sonoma Mission Inn for three nights and returned and found a very happy Emma waiting for us.

"How was she?" I asked Nick.

"Emma? C'mon, she's my pal. She's always a good girl." I handed Nick a fifty dollar bill and thanked him. Nick feigned a refusal of the money but deep down inside appreciated the gesture. He was an occasional actor and as of late the roles were far and few between.

I carried our bag inside. Julie was understandably in a great mood. The first thing she wanted to do was tend to her rose bushes out back. These were her children. She would talk to them and spend an inordinate Amount of time with them.

Have fun," I said. I'll be in my office.

My office was actually a small nook off the living room. I set up a small desk there and a desk top computer. I sat down and logged into the secure server that I used to send "deals" to Raven.

I composed a brief message that read, "Urgent! Need to recall assignment to terminate Scott Butler. You will retain your fee. Please confirm."

I sat there staring at the computer. Julie entered the house and went into the bedroom to unpack. I walked into the kitchen to grab a can of Coke. I heard the bleep on my computer that sounded whenever I had a new email. I raced back to the computer and stared at the screen. It was a message from Raven whom I had never heard directly from in the past. The message had only five words, "Sorry, all sales are final." Although I wasn't surprised, my heart sank. Now what?

Twenty-Four

The San Francisco Chronicle's building stood proudly at Mission and Fifth in the South of Market area. Although owned by the Hearst Corporation, the paper was a ghost of its once majestic self. At one time it was one of the shining lights of the Hearst Empire, but in recent years there had been massive layoffs in all departments, including editorial that left the paper in dire straits. One of the surviving bright lights at the paper was investigative reporter Elizabeth Harris. Juicy investigative stories tended to sell paper hence the fragile job security she found herself enjoying.

She had moved to San Francisco four years ago from Chicago where she had been on the staff of the Chicago Tribune. Friends doubted the wisdom of her move leaving one of the country's great newspapers, but the early warning signs were there in Chicago. The competitor, the Chicago Sun-Times, has just signed for bankruptcy and it was rumored that the Tribune wasn't far behind. She had been offered a position with a good, not necessarily great, newspaper at a very good salary, plus the opportunity to live in San Francisco where she had visited several times each year and always wanted to live there.

At exactly five foot three she was not an imposing figure. She had shoulder length dark hair, big brown eyes, and a knowing smile. However, when she entered a room she was bigger than life. Nobody messed with Elizabeth Harris.

One of the first things she did when she arrived at the Chronicle was put in an anonymous tip line. At first she got resistance from management largely because of expense, but when she offered to pay for it out of her own pocket they caved and agreed to have it installed. Almost immediately it started paying dividends. One of the initial tips led to a series of stories about corruption in the Catholic Church in San Francisco. The tip line received almost fifty calls each week. Elizabeth carefully listened to each message. Some of them she immediately discarded. They were far-fetched accusations that just didn't make sense. Less than five each week cried out for additional investigation. Maybe one or two each month were candidates for stories

She sat down at her desk late Friday afternoon and started to retrieve the voice mail messages from the tip line. The first several messages were of no interest. One was from a crazy woman named Old Bess who phoned in worthless tips each day. Today's tip was that the mayor, a man, was really a woman cross-dressing. She laughed, erased it, and listened to the next message: "I'm sure you'll remember several weeks ago a body was found in the park in Sausalito with a bullet in its head. Inside the deceased's suit pocket was a list of high profile Sausalito residents including the Mayor and several city council members. This is well worth your investigation. Something like this just doesn't happen. This is no coincidence."

Elizabeth played the message back three more times and knew this was something worth her attention. She went to see Jack Arnold, her editor, and played the message for him. "Wow, looks like you've got a potential juicy story," he said. "Go for it."

She technically didn't need his blessing, but that always made it easier if she had his buy-in. She pulled out her Sausalito Ferry schedule and decided to take a ride over there to start snooping around. She knew a few people at higher levels in Sausalito but her contacts there were not deep. She found the next ferry was leaving in 35 minutes. She threw her pad in her over-sized black purse and headed out the door. It was a nine block walk to the ferry. She decided to walk and arrived at the Ferry Building with six minutes to spare. She paid $8.00 for a one way ticket and walked onboard the ferry, Marin. She grabbed a seat on the main deck inside and stared out the window. She hadn't had a home run story in quite awhile. This could be the story she had been hoping for.

A half hour later the ferry pulled into the ferry landing in Sausalito. She walked down to the lower level to get off the ferry. Walking the long approach towards shore she noticed about 100 people with their bikes getting ready to get on the ferry for a return trip to San Francisco. A company called Blazing Saddles rented bikes for a ride over the Golden Gate Bridge to Sausalito which came with a ferry ticket for a ride back,

Elizabeth walked through the large parking lot by the ferry landing towards the concrete elephants that stood at attention guarding the park. She wanted to see exactly where they had found the body of Vincent Check. Elizabeth took out her camera and took several photos. She next headed north on Bridgeway towards the Police station. She had been there before and knew how to divert off Bridgeway to find it set back on the east side of the street down a gravel road from Bridgeway.

The Police station was a large temporary building that had been in use a whole lot longer than most temporary buildings. She rang the bell outside and was buzzed in. A young female civilian employee was manning the front desk. "May I help you?" she asked.

"Yeah, my name is Elizabeth Harris. I'm with the Chronicle. I'm working on a story about the body that was found by the elephants a month or so ago. Who is handling that investigation?"

"That would be Officer Stacey Gordon. She's not in. Today is her day off. Would you like to leave a message?"

She handed the young woman a business card. "Please ask her to call me."

Elizabeth was disappointed that Stacey was not on duty today but not surprised. The Sausalito PD has not always been the most accommodating when she has worked on Sausalito stories in the past. She hoped that this time things might be different. She had to make friends with Officer Stacey Gordon.

She walked back towards downtown and caught a cab by the Casa Madrona Hotel and asked to be taken to the Alta Mira. "Are you sure?" asked the driver. Elizabeth explained that she was quite sure. Minutes later they navigated up the curvy streets of the hills behind the Casa Madrona and arrived at the Alta Mira. She paid the driver and left an especially generous trip feeling guilty that it was such a short trip and thus a small fare. Elizabeth entered the main building and this time found Helen foster herself at the front desk.

"Hello, I'm looking for whoever is in charge," said Elizabeth.

"That's me. My name is Helen Foster. I'm the Director."

"My name is Elizabeth Harris. I'm with the Chronicle. I'd like to talk to you about Vincent Check."

"Oh my, there certainly is a lot of interest lately about poor Mr. Check."

"What do you mean?"

"The Sausalito Police were just here a day or so ago."

"Let me guess, Officer Stacey Gordon."

"Well, how in the world did you know?"

"Just lucky I guess."

This visit was good for Helen Foster's ego. Imagine. A reporter actually wanted to spend time with her. Wow! She led Elizabeth back up to the same table where she had met with Stacey Gordon. The two women talked for almost two hours. Elizabeth found someone willing to answer and all questions, and she wasn't about to stop.

It was close to five, and Elizabeth knew there was a ferry back to San Francisco at 5:30. She thanked Helen Foster for her time, gave her a card, and asked her to call if she thought of anything. Helen promised she would do so. She called Elizabeth a cab which arrived minutes later. She made her ferry with five minutes to spare. Her mind was spinning. Helen Foster had given her a great foundation from which to start her story. What she hadn't found was the tie between Vincent Check and the elite of Sausalito.

She checked her voice mail. Stacey Gordon had already returned her call but wouldn't be available until the next day. That made her happy. The Sausalito cops were not hiding from her, at least not quite yet. She left Stacey a voice mail to call her back and thanked her for the quick response.

A half hour later she disembarked at the ferry Building and board the number 14 bus on Mission Street to get back to the office. There was still a lot she wanted to get done before heading home. This was an excellent first trip to Sausalito. She wanted to rewrite her notes and hopefully catch her editor, Jack Arnold, to bring him up to date on her trip.

As was her regular routine she checked the tip line before she left for home. The computer reminded her, "You have three messages.'

She played the first two which were more or less junk email, but the third was golden, "How was your trip to Sausalito? Here is a little hint. Although Vincent Check lived at the Alta Mira for several months he had neither an alcohol nor drug addiction. So why was he there?" More later.

Her adrenalin started flowing. "Holy crap, I have my own Deep Throat," said exclaimed. "Now how do I get through to this person?"

She changed the greeting on the tip line and added the sentence, "If you're the person who called in with the tip regarding the Sausalito story, please call me on my cell phone, 415-555-8692. I would very much like to speak with you as soon as possible. This will be a completely confidential call. Thank you."

Elizabeth checked her voice mail every half hour. Five hours later there were no further messages. This was driving her crazy. Patience was not one of her greatest virtues. However, a story of this magnitude needed patient thoughtful care. She had to get through to her source and get the entire story. This person obviously knows everything that is going on. This was an opportunity she could not squander. She worried what she would do if her source decided to not go any further. She wondered how she might search for this person if the informant suddenly became violent

Twenty-Five

The long Memorial Day weekend was coming up. Julie and I had no plans and I suggested that we go see her Mother and Father who recently moved to Southern California. Her parents are lovely people and live in Westlake Village, an upscale community in the west San Fernando Valley, about an hour directly west of LA. I didn't want to be a stationary target. I booked our flight to LAX on the Southwest Airlines website. We were set to leave the Thursday night before and come back the day after Memorial Day. Although I had no way of knowing I felt I would be safe for the weekend. I asked Nick to watch Emma and gave him the keys to my Jaguar and asked him feel free to use it while we were gone. He didn't have a car. He is so good to us, and I thought he'd enjoy it while we were gone.

We made arrangements with Marin Door-to-Door, an airport van service to pick us up at 7 AM for our 9:30 AM flight. We originally going to drive, but I thought this might be easier. The van arrived five minutes early. The driver came to our door and helped carry our bags to the van. There was another couple in the van, and we learned we were the only other passengers on this trip and luckily we headed direct to SFO. The traffic was light on the Golden Gate Bridge. We went through the toll plaza and turned on 19th street which six miles later turned into Highway 280. Ten minutes later we maneuvered onto Highway 380 which led to SFO. We arrived at the airport about 40 minutes after leaving Sausalito. The other couple got off first at the United Terminal. They said they were going to visit family in Omaha for the weekend. Los Angeles certainly sounded like the better family weekend. The van left them out at Southwest Airlines. I checked our bags at the curb. We went inside and breezed through security. We had printed our boarding passes at home and were able to proceed directly to our gate.

We got to the gate several minutes before boarding. I scanned the crowd in the terminal to see whether or not there was anyone out there who might be Raven. We were in the first group to board the plane and grabbed an aisle and middle seat near the back. I wanted to be rather inconspicuous and blend in with others. I succeeded.

I carefully examined every person who boarded the plane. My paranoia was running rampant and rightfully so. The flight to LAX was uneventful. We arrived at the gate in LA 15 minutes early. I was deeply concerned that Raven slipped on board with us. Of course Julie knew none of this and wondered why I appeared to be agitated.

We were the last people off the plane. The normal crowd at the gate had largely dispersed. The plane was going on to San Diego, and a small group of passengers had started to gather. I scanned the area around the gate and saw nothing suspicious.

"Scott, are you okay?" asked Julie.

"Yeah, I just have a lot on my mind. A few days down here in LA will be all that I need to feel better."

Julie's Mom and Dad, Sandy and Bill Warren, met us in the baggage area. Julie's Mom, now in her mid 60s, was still a head turner. Bill was tall and athletic looking. He had played football at Gonzaga. Our bags came down early. Bill grabbed one; I grabbed the other, and we headed out the door towards the vast parking garage that sat across the access road from the terminal. Bill had parked his

Lexus in a close-in spot, and soon we were on our way. Julie sat in the back with her Mom. Bill and I were upfront.

"So how was your flight?" asked Bill. We never had an awful lot to talk about, and this was his attempt at being engaging and polite.

"Nice and short."

He laughed. Bill's a printing salesman, and he proceeded to tell me about some new press his company just installed. I pretended to be both interested and impressed. I did my best to be polite. I looked in the back, and Julie gave me a knowing smile. Julie and her Mom talked about the needlepoint shop. Her Mom professed a desire to learn how to knit. Julie told her it would be her pleasure to teach her how and suggested she come up for a long weekend sometime soon.

About an hour later we arrived at the Warrens' home in Westlake Village. It was a beautiful ranch style home sitting on a large lot overlooking a lake. It was the perfect locale for her parents and a lovely place for us to visit. She was an only child and was lovingly spoiled by her parents over the years. This was the stereotypical All-American family.

Bill grabbed both bags and led us to the guest bedroom which her Mom had redone it is soft earth tones. The only remnant of Julie's childhood was a large desk sitting in one corner that had been her grandfather's desk at a Downtown San Francisco law firm.

As we unpacked I whispered in Julie's ear, "I'm so glad we came."

Sandy stuck her head in the room. "We thought we'd take you guys out to lunch," she said. Although we weren't really hungry we smiled.

"Sounds good," we replied in unison.

It was a short drive to Alex and Aldo's, a small Italian restaurant we had been to several times before. .Sandy and Bill were regulars there and were greeting accordingly like valued guests in one's home.

Bill ordered a bottle of his favorite cabernet, a musky favorite from Niebium-Coppola. We studied the menus. I chose the penne pasta with white clam sauce. Julie opted for the special, some kind of fish with pasta. It was nice to sit and relax. We had been through so much lately.

My cell phone rang. I excused myself from the table and stepped outside. I noticed on the caller ID the caller was Nancy Drew, my neighbor and Nick's landlady.

"Scott, there has been a terrible tragedy," she whispered, choking back tears."

"What's wrong, Nancy? Is Emma okay?"

"Emma's just fine. It's Nick. He's dead."

"Oh my God. What happened?" It hadn't sunk in what she had said. We had just seen Nick. How could he be dead?

She proceeded to tell me that Nick was making a run to the store in my car, and when he started my Jaguar there was a loud explosion.

The car caught fire, and Nick died instantly. The rescue squad came very quickly, and there was nothing they could do.

The bomb was obviously intended for me. Raven was at work.

This would be a hard one for me to live with. My friend, Nick Costello was dead. I went back to the table and told everyone what happened.

"Poor Nick," said Julie. She started to tear up. "He was such a wonderful person."

"How awful," said Sandy.

How awful indeed. I really had to stay on the top of my game. Raven was coming to get me. The fire salvo had been shot. Raven was not likely to miss again. I knew I was now a priority and near the top of Raven's "To Do" list. The question remained; did Raven know where I was this very moment? Did Raven realize the car bomb was for naught? Were Julie, I and her family in immediate danger? I felt anxious and helpless. It was difficult, but I tried to maintain an illusion that nothing was wrong.

Twenty-Six

It came as no great surprise when the next call to my cell phone was the Sausalito Police department. It was Officer Stacey Gordon. She sounded irritated to be calling me rather than being sympathetic for the loss of my car. I thought somebody had probably gotten her out of a party to call me.

"Mr. Butler, do you have any idea who in the world would want you dead and plant a bomb in your car?" she asked.

"As you can imagine, I am in shock," I lied. "I mourn for my friend Nick and I have absolutely no idea why anyone would wish me ill," I started sweating and had an uneasy feeling in my stomach.

"With all due respect, sir, I find that hard to believe. Somebody wanted to send you to meet your maker. We are dealing with the death of a much beloved citizen. You need to think about this further. This isn't something that just came out of the blue. Surely you must have some idea who wishes you harm. Something like this typically doesn't happen for the hell of it. We know you're representing the City of Sausalito in a law suit against the owners of the Alta Mira. Think this might have anything to do with you case? This is a high stakes game that you're playing."

"I swear I have no idea. I certainly can't think why anyone would do something so extreme like a car bomb to try and kill me." I was relieved that they were taking the investigation in another direction.

"When are you coming home?"

"We were planning on coming home Tuesday. Would you like me to come any sooner? I'll do whatever you want me to do."

"On the contrary. Stay as long as you like, however keep your cell phone on. You can rest assured that we want to continue talking with you."

I once again returned to the table.

"Who was that, honey?" asked Julie still shaken and looking concerned.

"The Sausalito Police. They were asking me about the bombing. They wanted to know if I could think of anyone who would want to hurt me."

"Do you? Had we driven to the airport like we were originally going to we'd both be dead right now."

Her parents remained silent. Her mother stroked Julie's hand.

"I have no idea. Yes, I'm shocked. Yes, I'm scared."

We finished our meal. No-one said a word. On the drive back to their house Bill tried to make small talk to no avail. I knew I was now in Raven's focus. Raven was doing the appointed task and wanted me dead. Raven probably has a good idea where I AM. The tendency might be to stay down here for awhile, but that would endanger the Warrens. I decided that we would go back on Monday. I was debating whether or no to come clean with the Sausalito Police but that would put me in a compromising position as someone who was complicit in the murders I helped facilitate. I was scared not only for my safety but Julie's as well. I didn't know what to do. Although putting a hit out on myself seemed an inspired move at the time it was without a doubt the dumbest thing I have ever done. I had created the biggest nightmare of my life.

I was very quiet all weekend which was very unusual for me. Julie knew this was bothering me but had no idea what the severity of the situation was. I went to bed early before Julie on Friday night. She was close behind, changed into my favorite nightie and snuggled up next to me. I turned away. I was a man possessed.

"Wow, I'm sorry," she said. "I thought this might make you feel better."

"I'm sorry, Julie. This had really shaken me up. I keep thinking of poor Nick. Had it not been for me he'd still be alive. I've got to find a way to live with that fact. Poor Nick It's my fault."

"Scott, it's not your fault."

If she only knew the truth.

Raven watched the Channel 5 News detail the shocking death of Nick Costello in Sausalito.

"Poor schmuck. Don't worry, Scott. I'm right on your tail."

Twenty-Seven

Stacey Gordon spent the next week interviewing everyone on the list. The response was the same, a combination of shock, outrage, and confusion. According to each individual none had ever had the pleasure of meeting the late Vincent Check nor did they have any idea why their name was on the slip of paper in his pocket. It was obvious that the group had met and decided to tell the same story. Everything sounded so well-rehearsed. They had developed their talking points and were sticking to them.

She agreed to meet that afternoon with Elizabeth Harris from the San Francisco Chronicle. She wasn't sure what to make of this request and frankly wasn't sure how much she should reveal about her investigation. She decided to give Elizabeth the benefit of the doubt and see what she had to say. She agreed to pick up her up at the ferry at 10:20AM that morning. Elizabeth was one of the first people off the ferry and walked over to Stacey who was standing by the ferry sign that listed the arrivals' and departures of the ferry.

"Officer Gordon?" asked Elizabeth as she approached Stacey.

"Please call me Stacey."

They walked along the row of tourist shops towards the Winship Restaurant. They entered and grabbed a secluded table near the back. Stacey immediately liked her. She seemed both extremely competent and friendly.

After the obligatory small talk Stacey asked, "So what do you know about the whole situation regarding Vincent Check?"

My tip line received a call from someone who told me there was more to the story that met the eye. I am told that in Mr. Check's pocket was a piece of paper with the name and phone numbers of several Sausalito residents."

"And what else?"

"That's about it right now. But you've got to admit finding a list of well known Sausalito residents in the pocket of an assassinated man with ties to the mob is unusual."

"So what do want from me?" asked Stacey. "What can I do to help?"

"Tell me what you can."

Stacey felt a rapport and decided to trust her. "I probably don't know much more than you do. It hasn't been an easy investigation. As you might imagine there are many powerful people who wish I would just shut up and go away."

Elizabeth stared out into the restaurant for a brief moment and said. "Stacey, this is a huge story. You help me and tell me what you can without compromising your investigation. I will in turn do the same for you."

"Everything we talk about never comes back to me. Okay? I want to be an anonymous source. That's very important. I have fought hard to be a trusted member of my department."

"Deal. My lips are sealed. Don't worry. I am very discreet."

Stacey went on to walk her through her frustrating series of meetings with everyone on the list. "Not one person had any idea how their name got on the list. This all so mind boggling."

"The existence of this list was never revealed in the media, was it" asked Elizabeth.

"No, but rumors have been flying freely. It's almost like a badge of honor to be on this list. Crazy huh!"

"Is there anyone on the list that has particularly perked your interest?"

"Yeah, a couple folks. First of all, his honor, the Mayor, Mike Long. He was a little bit too smooth when I spoke with him. It was almost as if someone had crafted his answers for him. The other person is Sid Emmett, a semi scumbag who runs the local newspaper. He was just the opposite from Long. He was unbelievably nervous. I thought he was going to pass out at any moment. Of course none of this may mean a damn thing but who knows."

"I think it's time to reveal the existence of the list, said Elizabeth. "It's time to go public."

"Do what you want," said Stacey. "Just leave my name out of it. "

"Of course. You will be the prototypical 'anonymous source'"

Elizabeth took a photo of Vincent Check out of her purse and showed it to Stacey.

"Where did you get that?" asked Stacey. She was surprised to see a photo of him still alive.

"Helen Foster from the Alta Mira sent it to me."

"It's strange that you mention her name. She has disappeared. She hasn't shown up for work in three days. No-one has seen her. We are out looking for her. She's been missing in action from work, and no-one has seen her around her apartment complex here in town as well."

"Wow. This gets more interesting all the time."

Stacey put a five dollar bill on the table and said, "Let me leave first so no-one sees us leave together. We don't need anyone to know about this meeting."

Elizabeth shoved the bill back at her. "No, this one is on me. Stay in touch."

She paid the check and left a generous tip. She decided to stop at local businesses to see if anyone recognized Vincent Check. Crossing the street she walked to the corner and stopped in Sausalito Jewelers where a young woman was cleaning the glass display cases with Windex. The young woman stared thoughtfully at the photo for a minute and replied she could be of no help.

Elizabeth then stopped at the clothing store right around the corner and the response was the same. She got a similar answer from the next three shops but was lucky when she stopped into the famous

No-Name Bar. Harry, the bartender, said that he had seen Check in the bar on several Sundays.

"Are you sure?" she asked.

"Positive. Is he in trouble? He drank vodka and tonics."

"Not anymore. He's dead."

She thought that it was ironic that the first person to recognize the photo of a man enrolled in a very expensive alcohol rehab program was a bartender.

Walking down the block she stopped by the valet booth at the Casa Madrona. Kevin, the head valet, was on duty. He looked at the photo and recognized it right away. "Sure, I know this guy. Used to park with me on Sundays. Has a big black Lexus. He's always tip me 50 bucks. That's a good way to have someone remember you. Nice guy. I think his name was Vincent."

Elizabeth had been told that the only days residents in the Alta Mira program were allowed to leave was Sundays. This was all making perfect sense.

She knew The Marin Times newspaper was located in an old historic building north on Bridgeway not quite as far as the Police station. She stopped in and asked if Sid Emmett was available.

"May I tell him who's here to see him? By the way, do you have an appointment?" asked the matronly-looking woman at the front desk.

"My name is Elizabeth Harris. I'm with the San Francisco Chronicle."

The woman disappeared and Sid Emmett came out a few minutes later. He thought Elizabeth was looking for a job.

"No, but thanks for asking" she said. "I'm working on a story about the strange death of Vincent Check. Do you have a few minutes to talk? Or would another day be better?"

Sid was at a loss for words. "I am quite busy right now. I'm up against deadline. I'm sure you understand."

"I understand, of course, but do you have even five minutes?"

He led her into his cluttered office. He cleared a pile of old newspapers off a guest chair and invited her to be seated.

"I will only take a minute, Mr. Emmett."

"Please call me Sid."

"Okay, Sid. The late Vincent Check was found with a bullet in his forehead lying in the park. In his pocket was a slip of paper with your name on it. Any idea what your name was doing in the pocket of a dead man with ties to the mob'

He turned pale. "I have been told this was the fact but know nothing about it. Now if you'll excuse me. I never met the man and it's highly doubtful he knew who I was.

"Of course." She handed him a business card. "If you think of anything give me a call."

He showed her the door, thanked her for stopping by, hurried back to his office, and shut the door. He picked up the phone and dialed Mike Long's cell. He didn't answer, and Sid left a voice mail. "Mike, some broad from the Chronicle stopped by. They're working a story about Vincent Check and the list of names in his pocket. What the fuck are we going to do?"

Mike Long got the voice mail message and chose not to return it. Sid Emmett was not surprised. Long thought Emmett was somewhat of an embarrassment and frankly wanted as little to do with him as possible.

At one time Emmett though Mike Long could do no wrong. He was starting to see this was not the case. Mike Long was out for himself and only himself. Everything else in his life was secondary, his wife, his friends, Sausalito, everything. Mike Long would do whatever he had to in order to benefit himself. He didn't care who he had to step over to do so.

Twenty-Eight

The last thing I had on my mind was trying to develop new clients. However, my friend Arnie in Palo Alto asked me to see a former colleague of his who was fighting a patent infringement case against another Silicon Valley company. I agreed to take him to lunch. Intellectual property was not my specialty, but I knew enough about it to be able to recommend someone who really could help him. I made a reservation at Poggio and asked him to meet me there at 11:30AM. I always liked to get an early jump on the lunch crowd. I got there a few minutes early and was greeted minutes later with my Grey Goose martini. The guy I was meeting for lunch was named Mark Bohlman. You could tell he didn't work in Sausalito. He was wearing a sincere black pin-striped suit and lace-up oxford shoes. He looked more like a banker or attorney than an entrepreneur out of Silicon Valley.

I stood up to greet him and invited him to have a seat. We were in my usual table by a large window in the back. It was good for both getting some sun and girl watching. He explained that he had proprietary new software for airline scheduling and that another company had reversed engineered the product and was now offering something almost identical. He explained in great detail how the software worked. I pretended to understand what he was saying but had no idea. We studied the menus. I ordered the special, a seafood stew. He ordered the red snapper. He passed on a cocktail and ordered a bottle of Amstel Light.

I explained to him that I probably was not the right person for the assignment; however I wanted to refer him to Ray Starling, a classmate of mine at Cal who is one of the top intellectual property attorneys in the country. I promised to have Ray call him as soon as possible." I'll see if he can get to you this week."

Our lunch arrived. "Gee, your stew looks good," Mark said. "I wish I would have ordered that."

"Tell you what," I said, "my office is 30 seconds away. I can have this any time I want. Why don't we swap?"

"I couldn't do that."

"Nonsense." I grabbed his plate and gave him my stew.

He enjoyed the stew the way someone might enjoy a fine glass of wine, deliberately and with respect. We barely said a word while enjoying our lunch.

"How is it?" I asked.

"Wonderful, absolutely wonderful. Thank you so much."

We decided to be good and pass on desert. He offered to pay for the meal. I refused and gave our server, Tanya, my Platinum American Express Card. While she was away we talked golf, a common passion, and agreed that we would get our mutual friend, Arnie out on the links sometime soon.

"Got to be careful playing with Arnie," he laughed." He cheats."

"Don't we all just a little bit."

I made sure he got his parking ticket validated and walked him over to the valet by the Casa Madrona Hotel. The valet quickly retrieved his car, a hunter green range Rover. He thanked me again and we agreed to talk soon. I genuinely liked him and thought the prospect playing golf with him was a pleasant idea. I hoped we might be able to arrange this sometime soon.

I returned to my office and Checked email and voice mail. My Dad had called and wondered why I hadn't called in over a week. He was right on top of everything and could tell you always how many days between our phone conversations.

I promptly returned his phone call and accepted his scolding for not calling for a while. I decided to be the dutiful son and let him blow off some steam.

"No excuse, Dad," I pleaded. "Cut me some slack. Things have been crazy here." That was putting it mildly. I didn't tell him about my car and about Nick's death. That would have freaked him out. Even though I'm in my late 40s he still worried about every little thing dealing with my life. I suppose I'd be the same way if I had children. The less knew about anything the better.

Dad was in a sports-minded mood that afternoon. His beloved Chicago White Sox were back in first place and he was basking in its glory. "I'm happy for you and your team," I said.

"Yeah, this could be the year. I've been waiting for this since they won the World Series in 2005."

This was his standard line every year about this time of the summer when the Sox would suddenly get hot and later in the summer cool off and break his heart.

"Hope you're right, Dad," I said. "I'll fly in and take you to the World Series."

"Promise?"

"Of course, we'll even take Ted."

"That would make your brother so happy. I'm sure it would. We've got to get to that point before we get too excited and start booking airline reservations."

He laughed.

"Got to run, Dad. Give Mom a kiss for me. Love you."

I checked my other voice mail messages. Howie Steiner called. It sounded important, but then again Howie thought everything was of earthshaking importance. I decided to call him later in the day and have him come in tomorrow morning.

There was also an email from SAM Singer, the attorney representing the Alta Mira. I returned his call and he was out, thus beginning what I was confident would be an endless round of voice mail tag. I wish I would have had his cell phone number because I wanted to speak with him as well.

Also there was a voicemail from an investigator with State Farm Insurance. Apparently they were trying to find a reason to not pay the claim on my Jaguar that was now only a memory. You pay thousands of dollars over the years, and now when you really need them they were giving me a hard time. I would call him back the next day and stir up some trouble if they tried to stonewall me.

I decided to give Julie a call to just say hello. She answered the phone on the third ring.

"Sweetie pie, how are you?" I asked.

"My goodness, what do I owe this call? You don't normally pay me much attention during business hours. I'm flattered."

I laughed. "That's a nasty little habit of mine getting tied up in my work. I will change my ways."

"No need. I love you just the way you are."

"Hey, you in the mood for going out looking at cars tonight? I've got to replace the Jaguar."

"It all depends. Is a dinner date attached to car shopping?"

"Of course. I will come by the shop at 5, we'll go get your car and head out."

"Are we getting another Jag?" she asked.

"Perhaps, but let's look at other alternatives as well.

"How about that cute little BMW convertible we saw in Carmel? "Let's see what's out there, and you make the final decision." It was apparent there would be a BMW in our future. This had been such a good day that I almost forgot Raven was out there trying to kill me. I had no intention of making it easy for Raven whoever he or she was.

Twenty-Nine

The phone rang close to midnight. I was watching David Letterman. Julie was sound asleep on the couch. Emma was curled up on the floor next to her. A midnight call was seldom good news. I got a lump in my throat fearful something had happened to Mom or Dad. I gingerly picked up the phone, not knowing who was on the other end and why I was being called so late at night. The caller ID read "Private Number."

"Hello." I said softly as to not wake Julie.

"Scott, this is Arnie. Sorry to call you so late."

"Don't be silly," I said, "what's wrong?" I thought that Arnie might have been involved with a DUI incident. I had bailed him out once before when he had been arrested on a DUI.

"I just came from the hospital," he said choking back tears. "Mark Bohlman is dead."

"What? I had lunch with him earlier today. He looked to be in great shape."

"I know. He appears to have been poisoned."

My God, I had switched meals with him at lunch. The poison was meant for me. Raven was hot on my trail. I wasn't even safe at Poggio for lunch. How in the world did Raven come so close to pulling this off?

"That's horrible. We went to the restaurant where I eat every day, Poggio."

"I know. You've taken me there before. Lovely place."

The Palo Alto Police wanted your phone number. I expect you'll be hearing from them any minute."

Then I knew the Sausalito Police would be next. I felt bad for Mark's family and for John Legori who owned Poggio. Something like this had the potential close down his restaurant for good. This was something he obviously had nothing to do with.

Sure enough moments later the Sausalito called asking me if I would be "kind enough" to stop by the station at 9AM in the morning. I told them I would be happy to do so. I was sure that by now John Legori had heard from the authorities. I debated whether or not to call hi and decide to just stop by after I finished with the Police in the morning.

I ate at Poggio just about every day, so it was not difficult for Raven to know I would be there, but for her to get someone to put poison in my food and deliver it to my table would have involved some complicated action. I knew most of the kitchen staff as well. This just didn't make sense. I wondered if there was a new hire in the kitchen.

I hardly slept that night. I kept waking up thinking of poor Mark Bohlman. I decided I would call his family to express my condolences. This would be a very difficult thing to do as I knew the tainted food had been intended for me rather than him. Unfortunately there was no-one I could tell this to, certainly not the Police. I was holding some information that was vital to their investigation and for obvious reasons was unable to tell anyone. Here's another person who was dead because of me. Who might be next?

I could have predicted what would happen at the Sausalito Police the next morning. A portly bald detective named John McQuire led me into a small interview room and asked, "You seem to have a lot of excitement in your life lately, Mr. Butler. Why were you and the diseased having lunch yesterday?"

I explained to him that I am an attorney and Mark Bohlman was seeking representation.

"Did he hire you?"

"I told him I wasn't an expert in the field he needed, intellectual property and offered to make a referral to another attorney I knew who could help him more than I. It was a complex field that required a keen experienced mind."

"Did you?"

"I was very busy yesterday afternoon and was going to make the call today."

I didn't explain that we had swapped meals. The Police were still investigating the car bomb and I didn't want to send up another red flag. I knew that the Police were already thinking that there was no way this could have been a coincidence. A black cloud had formed over my head. I wondered how all of this would eventually end.

"How often do you go to Poggio?" he asked.

"Just about every day."

"Do you have any idea why someone would want to murder Mark Bohlman?"

"Considering that I just met him yesterday, I have absolutely no idea."

He continued with several more questions that I tried to answer o the best of my ability, but there wasn't much I could contribute. I certainly did not know Bohlman very well.

I walked towards downtown and stopped into Poggio to see John Legori. He was in his office in the back of the restaurant and stood when he say me coming.

"Scott, how are you?" he asked with a look of desperation on his face.

"I'm just fine, John. More importantly, how are you?"

"I don't know how this could have happened," he said. "Having a person die from poison after eating in your restaurant is horrific. I don't know what to do. The Police were here this morning and asked who was working in the kitchen yesterday and wanted me to make them available for interviews."

"What did you tell them?"

"I didn't say much of anything. I said that I would be happy to cooperate and set up times for them to meet with everyone who was working yesterday, both kitchen and wait staff."

"Good. Very good. When they question you just don't say too much. Do you have any idea who may be behind all this?"

"None whatsoever. Scott, this could close me down. Every penny I have in the world is invested in this place. You know that."

"We are not going to let that happen."

"Scott, would you be willing to represent me?"

My heart sank. I knew this was not something I could undertake. "John, I have a really full plate," I said. "However for the time being I will be happy to advise you and do whatever I can to help. In the meantime you need to find your own counsel. What about Walter Griddel, right here in Sausalito? He's pretty tough. I have gone up against him several times and haven't always won."

"Don't like him. He's an arrogant prick."

"Perhaps, but that's what you need right now. You're not looking for someone to pal around with. You need someone who will be an aggressive advocate."

"I need someone to help me through this nightmare. C'mon, Scott, can't you do this for me? I know you. I trust you."

"Believe me you'll be better served with someone else. If you decide to not hire Walter or if he doesn't have time to represent you let me know. I will find you representation. I promise."

He was facing a hell even more severe than he imagined. Normally I would have agreed to represent him but given the circumstances this was not something I could do. I felt bad, but that was just the way it had to be. I felt that suddenly I was letting down everyone in my life. This was a terrible feeling.

Thirty

The group of men gathered for lunch once again. This time the venue was Volare, an inconspicuous restaurant on Columbus in North Beach. They had bought out the restaurant for the lunch hour, and on the door was a sign that read, "Closed for Private Party." The restaurant's décor was pure Italian shtick, with red and white table cloths and pictures of famous Italian singers on the wall.

They were sipping cocktails and nibbling various Italian appetizers that were being passed. It was shortly after twelve thirty. Lunch would be served at one. Those in attendance had their choice of baked ziti or lasagna. Those who had been there before knew the baked ziti was the better choice. Even though smoking was illegal in San Francisco cigar and cigarette smoke filled the room. They were above worrying about such minutiae. If a cop stopped by they would slip him a couple hundred bucks to just go away.

Seven men were already there. They were expecting four more. The leader of the group had very low tolerance for those who were late and kept checking his watch. Two additional men walked in the door. Moments later the other two men arrived. They ordered their cocktails, two ordered scotch, the other two manhattans. They grabbed bruchetta off a silver tray a busty young woman named Amber was passing.

Precisely at one o'clock, the leader of the group took his seat at the head of along table. The others immediately followed suit. Lunch was served. Nine had wisely chosen the baked ziti; the others were left to suffer with a very pedestrian helping of lasagna.

The leader clinked his glass and spoke. "My friends. We've gone through a lot together… it's time to make our move on the Alta Mira. It's the most valuable piece of property in the Bay Area. We will gain control, level it, build condos and make lots of money. There's also the matter of the hidden gold. Unfortunately our original plan of having the dearly departed Vincent Check help in this transition didn't work. That's worthless little prick wound up working with competitive forces and we had to off him. All that being said, please enjoy your meal, and we'll talk more over coffee and dessert."

The tall man with the bulbous nose sitting next to the speaker. laughed and belched. He raised his glass and made a toast. "To our dear departed friend. Rest in peace."

Thirty-One

I became a man possessed. Raven was after me. She had tried twice to kill me and was not successful, leaving two innocent bystanders dead. I knew she would be trying again soon, and I had to keep moving.

I'm even getting to the point of being afraid to go to sleep at night, fearful that she might break in at night and kill me and possibly Julie if she got in the way. I called Bay Alarm and had them come out and install a top of the line alarm system in the house. I had even thought of getting a ferocious dog to help protect us, but I knew Emma was such a quiet and gentle soul and would not do well with another dog. Besides there are always ways to disable a vicious dog if they get in the way. Raven undoubtedly knew all the tricks.

Julie was becoming increasingly concerned with my mood and confronted me. "Scott, are you going to tell me what's wrong?" she asked. "You're walking around with a glazed look in your eyes," she said. "That's not like you. Are you going to level with me?"

I just smiled and said, "I have a lot on my mind." There was no way I could tell her what was really going on. She had to stay out of the ugly mess I had created.

"Do you want to talk about it?"

"No. It's something that I've got to work through by myself."

'Oh, c'mon. I thought we said we could talk about anything."

Not this. I know she was concerned about me, but I could not afford to come clean about my situation. I started to think about running, but did I want to leave everything in my world behind, my wife, my home, my practice?

I wondered if I could get into the witness protection program but realized that would be complicated and take much too long. If I did go away for awhile I was confident that Julie would be safe. The contract was on me, not Julie. I had to do something. I wasn't sleeping at night. I couldn't walk through town without thinking Raven was lurking on the street ready to terminate me. I still don't trust the barista named Tiffany who works at Starbuck's. She's a bit too flirty and always wants to know what's going on in my life. There's also a server named Matt at Poggio who tends to take care of me most days. Hey, maybe that's how the poison got into the food that was intended for me. My head felt like it was going to explode.

I even considered going back to the mob itself and tell them what I had done and plead for my life but knew that would be fruitless. We had a deal, a contract for services. As long as I continued to fulfill the contract my debt to the mob would be forgiven. If I did not fulfill our agreement they would kill Julie and me.

I started planning where I would go and more importantly how I would get there. I would either go to a location that had lots of people and lots of geography where I could disappear or retreat to a remote location where they would never think of looking for me.

After some detailed though I decided on the later. The question was now where would I go. At first I considered Santa Cruz, a tiny beach town about ninety minutes south of San Francisco. There were a number of small motels there where I could hide. How in the world would like ever know where I was hiding. However, Raven was very good at what he/she did and would not miss a third time.

My alternative idea would be to head up to Tahoe. It was extremely remote, and there all sorts of places I could go to hide. I would tell Julie that I was going to be on trial out of town and would be staying with a friend. We'd be able to be in contact every day on our cell phones. The question is where I would stay. Julie and I had talked for years about buying a condo in Tahoe but something always prevented us from doing something always came along that prevented us from doing so. One year we were ready to put an offer in on a condo in the Brockway area on Tahoe's north shore and suddenly our home in Sausalito needed a new roof and there went our down payment. The condo never happened, but it was something nice to dream about. Maybe someday.

Julie and I stayed several times at a small B&B called Tahoma Shores on the west shore of Lake Tahoe. It was a quaint property with fifteen small cabins, each with a distinctive name like "Tree House," "Bird's Cage," or "Berry Patch." The last time we were there we stayed in Berry Patch. Tahoma Shores was certainly a possible place for me to go and hide. I'm sure the owners would let me quietly register and remain anonymous. I just needed time to process everything that was going on in my life and figure out how to save myself.

Although Tahoe appeared to be the favorable alternative I had not yet made up my mind. Part of the equation would be figuring how to slip out of town without anyone, yet alone Raven know I was gone and certainly not where I was going. However, I knew that whatever I would decide to do I had to move quickly or there might not be a tomorrow. With reference to time there could be no margin of error.

First, I had to establish my cover story. A close friend of mine from college, Roy Weigand was practicing law in San Diego. Like me he's a litigator and a damn good one at that. I decided to call Roy and see if he would be willing to cover for me. I was sure that he would. I would call him the next day and was almost certain Lake Tahoe would be my destination.

I was confident I would be safe in Tahoe and would figure out a way to get there that would be hard for Raven to track. While in Tahoe I would figure out how to get out of this mess once and for all. I kept coming back to the idea of going to the Police and pleading for their mercy and understanding. This might be the only way. Even if they took me into custody I would still be alive.

Thirty-Two

We got distracted by the tragic death of Mark Bohlman and never got around to looking for a car to replace the Jaguar. I made it home from the office early as promised. Julie had on a cute little pink sun dress and was waiting at the door. She gave me a kiss and a hug and said, "I've been looking forward to this. How about if we grab a bite to eat before we go look at cars?"

"Deal. Where do you want to go?"

We decided on Piatti's, a lovely Italian restaurant, one entrance north in Mill Valley. We were headed north anyway towards San Rafael where all the car dealers were located so Piatti's was right on the way. It was shortly before 5:30 .PM, and happy hour was just beginning. The locals who made this their daily watering hole were gathering. Julie and I were led to a table by the large windows in the back of the restaurant that overlooked a small man-made lake. I gazed at her face and realized how much I loved her even after all these years. She hadn't changed much since her 20s and was possibly even more beautiful than she was then. We hadn't had much time to sit and talk lately, and I was looking forward to catching up. Sitting here made me realize more than ever why I didn't want to die. I loved this woman with all my heart and soul. We had such an almost perfect life together.

Julie had some new plans for the needlepoint shop that she was anxious to share. It continued to surpass even our most optimistic expectations as to what kind of business it would generate. Julie was spot-on when she sold me on the idea of setting up this shop. She wanted to start offering a full curriculum of classes for people who wanted to learn how to knit or to learn more advanced techniques. Not only would she derive income from tuition but from the purchase of material as well. I told her that I was behind this idea one hundred percent and felt it would be very successful. She also needed some additional funds to buy more stock. I gladly agreed to help her on that front.

This would have been a perfect time to tell Julie about the whole mess regarding Raven and beg her forgiveness, but I decided not to. I wanted her to not have any involvement whatsoever with the horrific adventure I found myself involved with.

Our server came to the table and took our drink order. Julie asked for a Cosmo. I ordered my usual Grey Goose Martini. I grabbed her hand and told her how much I loved her.

"My goodness, what brought that on, Scott?"

"I don't tell you that enough, and I should. I am crazy about you."

Julie blushed and said, "I love you too, Scott."

I did my usual survey of the room looking for anyone that might be Raven. I felt we were probably safe here. I couldn't see Raven trying to kill me in such a public place.

Our server came by once again and asked if we had any questions about the menu. We didn't. We were regulars and knew the menu quite well. We placed our order. Julie ordered the Fettuccine Alfredo. I opted for a chicken dish that was one of the day's specials. Both of our meals were good, and we passed on dessert to enable us to make our way up to San Rafael to look at cars. First we went to the Mercedes dealership and drove a two seat convertible. "Why do we need a full back seat?" I asked. "It's not like we ever schlep anyone around in the back seat." She agreed. A kind man named Carl was our sales person. I liked him a lot. Not once did he ask me what he'd have to do to earn our business. We told him that we were going to look at BMWs as well. He thanked us for stopping in and told us he hoped he'd see us again.

It was still early and we drove Julie's Crossfire to the BMW dealership right down the street. Although it was out of our price range we test drove a BMW 650. With a price tag of over $90,000, it drove like a dream, but we were not prepared to make this kind of investment. We drove a black convertible, and Julie and I laughed so hard our sides hurt. I had a great life which I didn't want to lose.

On our way home Julie reminded me that we did not have dessert and that she was still a bit hungry. We made our way once again and pulled into Strawberry Village, a large strip mall anchored by a new Safeway and several smaller stores and restaurants. There was a great yogurt shop around the back, and we pulled right up to the front door. Julie stayed in the car while I went in and got our usual. As I got out of the car I looked around hopeful Raven was nowhere in sight.

As we drove home, I decided to tell Julie that I would be soon heading to San Diego to help Roy Wiegand with a trial. I hated like hell lying to Julie, but I had no choice.

"I'm sorry, honey," I said. "I shouldn't be gone more than a week to ten days."

"That's an awful long time," she protested. "Why didn't you tell me about this earlier?"

"I just found out. His second chair bailed, and he had to fins someone quickly."

"When do you have to leave?"

"I'm not sure. I should know some time in the next day or so. I'll have my cell with me and we can talk any time you want. I'll be accessible 24/7."

She squeezed my hand and finished her yogurt. I could see her tearing up.

The next day I had serious work to do. I had to plan my exile. Where would I go? Where would I stay? How would I get there without Raven knowing where I was going? This all had to be very carefully orchestrated. There was no margin for error. No detail was too small to be forgotten. I was fighting for my life.

Thirty-Three

Tuesday was Stacey Gordon's day off. Elizabeth Harris invited her into the City for lunch. At first Stacey didn't know what to make of this invitation but graciously accepted. She hadn't been to the City for a long time. Rather than drive over the Golden Gate Bridge Stacey decided to take the ferry from Sausalito. She hadn't taken it in year and was looking forward to the half hour ride over to the Ferry Building. She got to the Ferry Landing in Sausalito about 15 minutes before the scheduled departure time and waited in a line of mostly tourists. When she boarded the ferry boat, Marin, she bought her round trip ticket on the lower deck and walked up a skinny staircase to the main deck where she knew she would disembark from once they reached the Ferry Building.

She grabbed a seat by a table near the window. The snack bar was already open, and she marveled at how much alcohol was already been served before noon. The ferry was operated under the arm of the same organization that was responsible for the Golden Gate Bridge. It largely ran at a loss and was supported by the high toll, now $6.00 for the privilege of driving over the bridge. There were about a dozen crossings each day between the Ferry Building and Sausalito. For the nine to five'ers, it was a very pleasant and civilized way to get and forth to work. The ferry sailed promptly at 11:10 AM for the 30 minute crossing. It was an unusual calm and sunny day on San Francisco Bay. The ferry sailed on the east side of Alcatraz where Stacey saw a boat full of tourists getting ready to start their tour of the famous prison. She hadn't been on this tour in years and thought it might be fun to take the tour again.

The ferry docked in San Francisco exactly 30 minutes after it left Sausalito. Stacey was waiting in line to get off when the giant door on the boat opened allowing the 103 passengers on to the ramp leading down from the boat. As Stacey passed through the exit from the landing area she deposited her ticket in the tall box. Elizabeth had told her to walk over to Mission Street and take the number 14 bus which would drop her off in front of the San Francisco Chronicle Building. When she walked to the bus stop she found the bus waiting. It took less than 15 minutes to ride down to Mission and Fifth, where she got off at the bus stop across the street from the Chronicle.

Stacey crossed the street and entered the Chronicle building. She asked the receptionist to please tell Elizabeth Harris that Stacey Gordon had arrived. Minutes later Elizabeth appeared and greeted Stacey, "I am so glad you could come down, Let me show you around and then we'll go to lunch."

Elizabeth walked Stacey through the newsroom. "Not very fancy," said Elizabeth.

"I think it's fascinating," replied Stacey. "So this is where it all happens."

"Ever been to Lefty O'Doul's?" asked Elizabeth.

"Where?"

"Lefty O'Doul's. It's a place out of San Francisco history. It'd kind of a bar, and it's kind of a restaurant. It's hard to explain. It's about a 10 minute walk."

"Let's go. Sounds like my kind of place."

They headed down Fifth Street and made the jog over to Powell Street by the Cable Car turnaround and headed towards Union Square. Moments later they arrived at Lefty's, which was on Geary, three doors west of Powell. Walking through the door was like entering a time warp and looking at an establishment from the 1950s, which was exactly when Lefty's was opened.

As you entered, on the left was a long bar with every seat filled and a very attentive woman bartender taking care of the crowd and sharing wisecracks. On the right was a cafeteria line where you could get everything from a roast turkey dinner with mash potatoes to a salad. The owner of Lefty's preferred to call this "haufbrau style" dining, but it was a cafeteria line. Plastered over the dark wood walls was every conceivable kind of sports memorabilia from actual balls and bats to photos of sports celebrities. Of course, there were many photos of Lefty himself who had started this restaurant in the early 1950s. In a prior life Lefty had been manager of the San Francisco Seals, a much beloved minor league team and had been favorite son, Joe DiMaggio's, first manager. The food at Lefty's was good, not great, but dependable. You always knew you could come in hungry, leave happy, without spending a lot of money. It was the kind of place that on any given day you might see the CEO of a large corporation or a laborer taking time off the job for a quick lunch.

Stacey went through the line first and ordered a roast beef sandwich on sour dough bread. Elizabeth ordered the day's special, beef stew. They walked to a booth near the back of the restaurant and sat. After some initial small talk Elizabeth spoke. "I think I have an idea what's going on."

"What do you mean?"

"I'm continuing to be contacted by an anonymous source who keeps feeding me information."

"Any idea who it might be?

"I think it's someone who was on the list in Vincent Check's pocket when he was found lying dead in the park."

"Why do you think so?"

"My source just knows too much to be an outsider. However I'm not sure."

Elizabeth went on to explain that her source told her that the men on the list were involved with a clandestine attempt to gain possession of the Alta Mira, the most valuable piece of real estate in Sausalito. One thing she didn't know was what was the involvement of the late Vincent Check in the whole operation. Once she figured that out she felt everything would fall into place.

"I think it's time for me to interview everyone on the list once again. Maybe I'll start to wear them down. It's strange that none of them wanted a lawyer present when I spoke with them."

"Don't do anything yet. I AM going to break this story next week in the paper. I have a feeling the folks on the list will start coming to you looking for some kind of deal."

"So you have no idea who your source might be."

"I do but too early to go public with my thinking. If you have any ideas follow your instinct. I promise you'll be the first to know if I find out anything else."

Stacey was fascinated by what she had just heard. She was aware of the public uproar about the Alta Mira but hadn't put two and two together to figure out this and the death of Vincent Check to be related. She wondered if Mayor Mike Long might be Elizabeth's source but quickly dismissed that idea. Long appeared too intelligent to suddenly turn on friends in such an operation. Could it be Sid Emmett? Perhaps. However, she thought he might not be smart enough to do something like that. She would carefully go over her notes from the extensive interviews she had conducted and see if anything stood out. She would also go back and carefully study the progression of the whole Alta Mira situation from the time it surfaced until now. She wanted to make sure she was well aware of everything that had happened and did not leave out any details. This was a very complicated matter that needed careful study.

The ride back to Sausalito was pleasant. Stacey sat on the open deck at the back of the ferry and enjoyed an iced tea. She started to plot out her next steps. She decided after all to go see Mike Long. It was a long shot that he would reveal anything but it was worth a try. When the ferry docked and she got off the boat she went over to a bench in the park adjacent to the ferry landing and sat. She pulled a small notebook out of handbag and looked up Mike Long's number. She punched in the numbers on her Blackberry and wasn't surprised when she got Long's voice mail. She left a message. "Hello, Mayor

Long. This is Stacey Gordon of the Sausalito Police. Would you be kind enough to call me? My cell is 415-555-2390. Thank you." She didn't expect a callback.

Thirty-Four

I sat down at my computer and started to plan my escape to Tahoe. I was confident this was the right thing to do. I would tell Julie I was down in San Diego helping my friend Roy Weygand in a trial as I knew he would Roy agreed to cover for me no questions asked. While in Tahoe I would figure out what I had to do to stay alive. More importantly I had to make sure nothing happened to Julie. She was truly an innocent bystander. Right now I valued her life more than my own. I had to very carefully protect her.

First I pulled up the website of Tahoma Meadows, the wonderful little B&B that Julie had stayed at several times. I made a reservation to arrive in three days on Saturday. I asked that they keep my reservation confidential and not acknowledge that I am coming or that I am actually there once I arrive. They apparently were used to requests such as this as no questions were asked. Their response was a simple, "No problem."

Now there was the question of how I would actually get there without drawing any attention to where I was going. I had carefully looked at my options. When most people go from the Bay Area to Tahoe they tend to drive. Unless you go over a holiday it's about a four hour drive. I had made the drive countless times and thought I would make myself more vulnerable if I was to spend a significant Amount of time in a car. Besides we had still not replaced the Jaguar. For all I know Raven may have planted a GPS device on Julie's

Crossfire. I didn't want to leave her for a couple weeks without a car. I had to come up with another idea.

Next I looked into chartering a private plane to fly me to Tahoe but the cost was prohibitive, and I wasn't all that certain how safe it would be. There was one pilot, an old-timer named Doc Cooper who had a seaplane that I could have caught in neighboring Mill Valley and flown up to Tahoe and land just about any place I wanted on the lake. I had called Doc Cooper and found he was already booked on the day I wanted to go. I had to come up with still another alternative idea.

I then decided to make it really easy on myself and take Amtrak to Sacramento and catch a bus to Tahoe. There was not an Amtrak train station in San Francisco. The closest train left from Emeryville, a small city directly over the Bay Bridge. Amtrak had a small office by the Ferry Building in San Francisco. A bus left there every couple hours for the Emeryville train station. I booked by Amtrak ticket on line for the upcoming Saturday. My train leaves at 1:30 .PM. I will take the ferry over from Sausalito in time to catch the bus for Emeryville that leaves at noon. I will tell Julie that I am catching BART, our version of the NY Subway from the Ferry Building to SFO.

I needed to get away to clear my head and decide on a course of action. Each day I lived in terror and knew I could not go on much longer like this. I had to move deliberately while being thoughtful. I was running for my life. What was ironic was the fact I had brought all of this on myself. Had I had not put out the contract on myself none of this would be going on. I had created my own nightmare. My clients always relied on me to solve their problems, and now I couldn't solve the biggest problem of my own life. I knew I had to dig down even deeper.

Thirty-Five

A thunder bolt hit Sausalito on Friday. On that day Elizabeth Harris published the first story in a series on corruption in Sausalito. It ran on the front page of the San Francisco Chronicle. The headline read, "The Mob and Sausalito City Fathers Involved in Scheme to Take Over the Alta Mira."

When the story broke the prior evening on the Chronicle's website phones started buzzing all over Sausalito. The story set forth the previously unannounced fact that when the late Vincent Check was found stone cold dead in the Downtown Sausalito park in the shadow of the concrete elephants he had a slip of paper in his pocket with the name and phone numbers of various Sausalito dignitaries including the Mayor, Mike Long and all City Council members. Although no-one was yet able to put the equation together it was known that Vincent Check was a member of the Chicago mob and had been a resident at Alta Mira. The land that the once great resort sat on was among the most coveted in Sausalito. It was speculated that the mob and the city fathers were working in tandem to take over the Alta Mira. Harris concluded that the case was under close investigation and that information would be shared in the newspaper as it became available.

Stacey Gordon had put her daughter Natasha down for the night and sat down at the computer, as was her custom to surf the Web. She wasn't much into television and found the Internet far more entertaining. As usual she went to sfgate.com, the website of the San

Francisco Chronicle. Right there on the home page was Elizabeth Harris' story.

"Holy crazy," she exclaimed, "She actually went ahead and did it. She read through it carefully and was relieved, per a solemn promise, that her name would not be connected with the story. The typical line, "According to a source familiar with the case..." was used. Moments later her phone rang. It was the Chief of Police. She wasn't surprised to get this call.

"Stacey," he sternly said, "have you seen the Chronicle's website?"

"Just looking at it now."

"And?"

"I have no idea who her source is. I certainly didn't tell her."

"Then how did she find out?"

"I met with her once, a brief meeting. Didn't get into any specifics at all." She hated to lie to her Chief but she was already deeply involved, perhaps too much so, and had to maintain her cover.

On the other side of town Mike Long was getting ready to sit down to watch Sportscenter on ESPN when the phone rang. It was Sam Holman, City Manager. In Sausalito, the City Manager was actually the chief operating officer of the city, while the Mayor was more of a ceremonial position aimed at generating good will and providing someone to chair city council meetings.

"Mike, this is Sam. Have you seen the Chronicle?"

"No, why?"

"Pull up their website, Mike. There's a huge story in there about corruption in Sausalito. Read it and call me back."

Not too pleased to be missing Sports Center he turned on his computer, waited for it to boot up and called up sfgate.com.

"Oh my God! He exclaimed. "Is this the beginning of the end?"

Moments later the phone rang again. It was Sid Emmett.

"Yes, Sid, I've seen the Chronicle. How did they find out? I have no idea. I need to have you help me call the others. If you can call Rhonda and Jim Squires that would help a lot. The message is very clear. If the Chronicle calls, which they will, we have no comment. When the Police come calling again it will be more serious, and we need to have an attorney present. We absolutely cannot speak to the authorities without counsel present."

"Who do you have in mind?"

"Not sure. One thing I do know is that it probably shouldn't be the same person for all of us. That would make us look as guilty as hell.'

"What about Scott Butler?"

"No. He's not the right guy. His client is the city in the action against the current owners of the Alta Mira. Besides he's not a criminal defense attorney."

"Criminal defense?"

"Don't be stupid, Sid. They're going to come after us with all guns blazing."

Several minutes later, a crew from CBS5 showed up on Mike Long's doorstep, followed by KGO-TV. Long politely turned them away indicating that at this time he had no comment on the matter. Moments later the trucks from KRON-TV and NBC Bay Area arrived. Long sent them away as well. They hung around and refused to leave. He has thought to call the Police but knew there was nothing they could do to deny the media access. He feared the trucks might still be there when he got up in the morning, He was right. They were still there waiting for a comment from Long.

At 11.PM, as was his custom, he turned on CBS praying nothing would yet be on the air. Unfortunately it was the lead story. The news crew that he had turned away from the CBS station found a sympathetic person in City Manager, Sam Holman, who said this was the first he had heard of the situation and that a complete investigation would begin first thing in the morning. He had already called Assistant City Attorney Kate Foster to request a meeting at 7:30 the following morning in his office.

"I am just a shocked about this as anyone. I do want to promise the citizens of Sausalito that we will find out the truth and justice will be answered. I do want to remind everyone that the individuals named by the Chronicle are innocent until proven guilty." The worst thing Holman did when assuming office 18 months ago was to give his cell number out to all Sausalito citizens and encouraged everyone to call him day or night with problems. That night he counted 79 calls from the time the time the story hit the Chronicle website until he finally decided to turn the phone off at 1:15AM. The citizens were outraged. So was he. The next day would be an interesting one to say the least. There would be a lot of questions asked for which he had no answer. He was a decent man who recently assumed this position coming from another city in the East Bay. He had no idea what the old guard of Sausalito had been up to. His own personal nightmare was just beginning. It would be up to him to right the ship. He knew he couldn't do everything on his own but had no idea who he could trust. Were there other people involved in the scandal whose names were not in Vincent Check's pocket? He had no way of knowing.

Thirty-Six

I spent the morning packing. Although I had no interest in wearing a suit while up in Tahoe, I packed two to complete the illusion that I was actually going to be on trial the next couple weeks. This would force me to travel with a second suitcase which I hated to do. I had to remember to complete each outfit with a couple dress shirts and ties. What a waste of effort, but needed. I also packed an ample supply of casual clothes, filling a second case with khakis, golf shirts, jeans, and sweaters. These are the clothes I knew I would be wearing every day.

Julie came up behind me and gave me a hug, "Do you really have to go?" she asked. "Not too late to change your mind."

"Afraid so. Hey, the two weeks will go by quickly."

"I'm really going to miss you. I hate when you are gone for so long. Even though we know you're healthy I still worry about you."

"I am really going to miss you too. Call me on my cell any time. I'm sure we'll talk a few times every day. You can always text me too, and I'll get right back to you."

Julie offered to drive me to SFO, but of course I declined. "There's no reason to do so. I'll just hop on the ferry and then catch

BART by the Ferry Building." Of course I wasn't telling the truth. In reality I would be catching the Amtrak bus for Emeryville to connect with the train for Sacramento. We would have to leave the house in about an hour and a half to drive down to the ferry terminal. This would be a difficult half hour to kill. There was so much I wanted to say but knew I couldn't.

"Why don't we take Emma for a quick walk before I go," I suggested. Julie grabbed the leash, hooked her up, and we headed up the hill. Like most dog owners we had the same route we followed every time we took Emma out for a walk. It was less than a mile long. We hardly said a word. I held Julie's hand while she held Emma's leash. I knew the next couple weeks would be especially tense. I tried to repress the thought that this might be the last time I'd ever see Julie. However, I was convinced that I had outsmarted Raven, or so I thought. This was way too complicated of an escapade for Raven to catch on to.

When we got back to the house I wrote Julie a letter and tucked it away safely in a spot where she would only find it if something happened to me. In the letter I told her how much I loved her and that I was sorry for the way things had turned out. I hoped she would never see this letter, and I planned to destroy it the moment I returned home from Tahoe.

About 20 minutes before the scheduled departure time of the ferry I grabbed my suitcases and told Julie it was time to go. She tried one more time to talk me into letting her drive me to SFO. I told her my way would be a lot simpler. for me just to jump on the ferry When we got to the ferry landing in downtown Sausalito she got out of the car and gave me a big hug and kiss. Her parting words were,

"Don't forget how much I love you." I left those thoughts imbedded in my mind. I boarded the ferry and decided to grab a seat on the lower deck. I parked my bags and went over and bought my ticket. I returned to my seat and stared out the window. I really loved my adopted city of Sausalito and hoped this would not be the last time I would be seeing it. I was doing what I had to do.

Moments later we pulled away from the dock. I debated whether or not to call Julie for a final so-long but decided against it. Exactly 26 minutes later we pulled up to the dock at the Ferry Building on San Francisco's Embarcadero. I was in no hurry to get off. My bus from the adjacent Amtrak Building bound for the Amtrak Station in Emeryville, right over the Bay Bridge, didn't leave for over an hour. I let most people off and then carried my two cases up to the main deck and rolled them down the access to the walkway. I deposited my ticket in the box by the exit and walked over to the Amtrak Building which was across the parking lot.

As I approached the desk I gave them my name. They punched in the computer and it yielded two tickets, one for the bus and another for the train. The bus wouldn't be leaving for some time. I grabbed a seat, took out my Blackberry and started checking my email. There was nothing important that needed immediate response. I also got up, gazed out the window, and wondered if Raven may have been following me. I quickly got my paranoia under control. Twenty minutes later the Amtrak agent announced that the bus for Emeryville would be arriving in ten minutes and please make our way to the curb. I grabbed my bags and did what I was told to do. There were 12 other people waiting with me for the connection to Emeryville. When the bus pulled up the driver opened the large doors on the side and put the entire waiting luggage inside. At first I was going to carry on my luggage on the train but decided that would be too awkward and decided to check it before I got on the train bound for Sacramento. It was a short ride to the station. It was Saturday and traffic was light on the Bay Bridge.

When we got there the train was just pulling up for a ten minute stop. I checked my bags and gave my ticket to a conductor for my assigned car. He gave me a seat on the upper level. "We're not too full today," he told me. "You should have an empty seat next to you for the entire trip." I thanked him and climbed on board. I hadn't been on a passenger train in over twenty years and was pleasantly surprised how nice it was. I sat down, sighed and wondered if I might be able to take a short nap between Emeryville and Sacramento. I decided not to. I didn't want to risk sleeping through my stop even though in was three hours away.

I grabbed the new copy of Vanity Fair from my briefcase and didn't get very far. I was distracted and had a difficult time concentrating. I took a walk on both levels of the car seeing if anyone remotely resembled who might be Raven. I soon realized that this was folly as Raven could be almost anyone. About 20 minutes after the train pulled away I got up and walked two cars to the front and found the club car. I found a seat and went down one level to buy myself a beer. I returned to my seat and mentally plotted what would happen the next few days. When I got to Sacramento I would purchase a bus ticket for Tahoe. The buses ran every couple hours and the arrival time of my train made it look like I would only have a short wait. I would get off the bus at the small bus station in Tahoe City and take a taxi to Tahoma Shores. It would only be a short taxi ride.

The train ride to Sacramento was uneventful. We made several quick stops along the way to drop off and pick up passengers and actually arrived in Sacramento 15 minutes early. I got off the train and once again looked to see if anyone who might be Raven was lurking around. For a moment I was concerned about a man in dark sunglasses that had been sitting the other side of the club car for most of my trip but was relieved when he was met at the station by his wife and kids.

I waited and was happy when I saw my two bags come by on the cart. I entered the building and waited for my bags to come down the carousel. I grabbed my bags and walked over to a ticket kiosk the opposite side of the station and bought my bus ticket for Tahoe City. The agent on duty told me the bus would be here in about 30 minutes. I found a seat on a nearby bench and patiently waited. Moments later I walked over to the snack bar and picked up a Coke. I was thirsty and knew it would be at least a few hours before I arrived at my destination.

The bus pulled up as scheduled and a group of tired looking passengers got off. They unloaded baggage out of the belly of the bus and then made the boarding announcement. I approached the bus, handed the driver my bags and my ticket and got on. I was glad to find a window seat near the front of the bus and hoped I would not have anyone sit next to me for the ride to Tahoe City. Bus rides were miserable, and the prospect of having an empty seat next to me made me happy.

Traffic was unusually heavy for a Saturday as we got on Highway 80 and headed up to Tahoe City. It was a beautiful day. The sun was shining, and I wished I had Julie sitting in the seat next to me, but not on this trip. I was literally running for my life and had to make some critical decisions that would affect our lives forever. The bus also stops in Truckee, a small quaint town about 45 minutes from Tahoe City. I debated whether or not to get off in Truckee and make my way to Tahoe on another bus just to confuse Raven but decided to stay on the bus I was currently on. I had no idea if Raven had any idea what I was up to but knew now was not the time to risk a damn thing. I had a carefully thought-out plan. I was confident Raven had not caught on to my plan. I had covered my tracks very well. I was starting to feel a bit better but knew now was not the time to get too comfortable or careless. I had to stay alert and at the top of my game. There was just too much at stake. I had no idea where Raven might be, but one thing I knew was that Raven was looking for me. It would have given me some comfort had I known if Raven was a man or woman. One thing I knew for sure was that Raven was extremely good at his or her trade. I would have to be even better at mine.

Thirty-Seven

As was her custom Elizabeth Harris checked her confidential hotline the moment she got to the office. The voice on the second message was the one she had been hoping to hear from. "Elizabeth, the time is now right for us to meet. I have many more things I want to share with you. Meet me tomorrow at 1.PM in the Grand Café in the Hotel Monaco. Don't worry about finding me. I know what you look like, and I will come to you. Grab a table, and I'll join you."

This message sent an adrenalin rush through Elizabeth's body. "Oh my God," she exclaimed.

"I had hoped this would happen." She ran over to her editor, Jack Arnold, and told him the good news.

"Just be careful, Elizabeth." he cautioned. "Whatever you're told we will have to verify before me print anything. This could be huge. Let's hope for the best."

Elizabeth called Stacey Gordon and told her the news. "I promise to tell you everything I find out," she told Stacey.

"Do you want me to do anything to help you prepare for this," asked Stacey.

"Nothing now. Just sit tight. I think I'm in good shape."

Elizabeth by nature was a very analytical person. She carefully considered who this mystery person might be as she had been doing all along. One thing she knew for sure that it was a man. It probably was someone from Sausalito and someone from the list of local officials found in Vincent Check's pocket at the crime scene. However, she wasn't sure. One thing she knew for sure was that in all likelihood she would have only have one shot to find out as much as possible from her informant. She sat at her desk and carefully committed to paper everything she knew about the scandal in Sausalito and figured out where the major holes were she had to fill in. She also had no idea how much time she would have with her informant and wanted to be both respectful and efficient.

She spent the majority of the day preparing for the meeting and even called Stacey Gordon to clarify a few things. She was anxious and wanted to make sure she left no stone unturned. It sounded like he was in a mood to talk. She had to take advantage of every minute they would spend together.

The day seemed to drag on forever. She had a hard time concentrating on anything other than her meeting the following day. She started working on a couple other projects to no avail. Her mind was locked onto the meeting the following day. She even blew off a couple staff meetings she had scheduled. She was in no mood to sit confined in a conference room.

That night at home she looked for things to do to help pass the time. She went for a run. That took her mind off things for a few minutes, but only a few minutes. She tried to watch an old movie on Turner Classic Movies but that only got her so far. She wasn't hungry but forced herself to down some pasta with a glass of red wine.

Shortly before ten o'clock an old friend of hers from college called. They talked for almost an hour. Elizabeth turned on the TV in her bedroom and tried to fall asleep. Sleep didn't come easily but she woke up at 3:10AM, turned off the TV and fell back asleep until her alarm went off at 6AM.

Elizabeth got out of bed, poured herself a bowl of Fiber One and made a pot of coffee. She decided to call into the office and see if there was anything on the tip line. She prayed that her informant hadn't changed his mind. The first message was from the informant. She held her breath and listened. "Elizabeth. I've decided to change the place we're going to meet. The Hotel Monaco is too mainstream I don't know if you know where the Park Merced neighborhood. It's out near San Francisco State. There's a small strip center near the entrance. On one end of the center is a small spot called Café Reina. I will meet you there at 1PM."

Elizabeth was relieved that the meeting was still on. She didn't care where it was. For a moment she thought of driving there but figure out it would be easier to take the Muni mass transit train to the West Portal Station and then cab it to Café Reina. The Powell Street Station was a short one block walk from the Chronicle. She got to the paper early that morning. She sat at her desk and reviewed her notes and then briefly touched base with her editor and headed out the door shortly before noon. The trains ran about every 15 minutes. The train ride to West Portal would take another fifteen minutes. She would get to West Portal in plenty of time to grab a cab and get to Café Reina early.

When she got to West Portal she found a couple cabs waiting. She told the driver where she wanted to go. "Yeah, I know that place," he answered. "They just opened. Really good coffee. The place hasn't gotten a lot of good buzz. Try one of the pastries. Reina makes them herself. Tell her Larry the cabbie dropped you off. Here's my card. Call if you need a ride back to the train."

Elizabeth arrived at Café Reina at 20 minutes to one. She ordered a latte and grabbed a table by the window. It was an adorable little bistro. Reina, whose name is on the door, is a beautiful young woman in her mid 30s. She was working behind the counter taking care of a throng of customers while her husband, Anthony was making the drinks. It was obvious why Café Reina was doing so well. The coffee and pastries were delicious and the owners were very friendly. They knew all the regulars by their first names. They were part of a giant apartment complex called Park Merced and were also adjacent to San Francisco State University.

Gazing out the window, Elizabeth nervously sipped at her latte. Several minutes later a non-descript sedan pulled up outside. A man in his mid- 60s stepped out of the car. There was nothing remarkable about him. He had on jeans, tennis shoes, and a black sweatshirt. He walked over to the counter, ordered a regular cup of coffee, and walked over and sat down with Elizabeth. He extended his hand and said, "Hello, Elizabeth. My name is Jeffrey Summers." This was a name she had not heard before. She was surprised. It was not someone from the list in Vincent Check's pocket.

"It's nice to finally meet you," she said. "I'm not sure where we should begin. Do you mind if I tape our conversation?"

"I'd rather you not. You never know if it might fall into the wrong hands. I hope you don't mind."

"That's fine," she replied taking her reporter's notebook out of her over-sized handbag.

"Before you ask any questions, why don't you just let me talk for a while," he said.

"Sure. Up to you. Talk as long as you like. I'm a good listener."

"I am kind of the go-to guy in Sausalito when someone needs something done. Granted frequently I push the limits of what's within the limits of the law. As you probably know one of the most valuable pieces of real estate in Sausalito is the Alta Mira. When the long time owner decided to retire and shut it down as a destination location there was quite the fuss among people who wanted to buy it. The insiders in the city more than anyone realized what it was really worth. When the owner decided to sell it to the people who are currently running the alcohol and rehab center Mike Long and his buddies were beside themselves. They thought they had a deal with the owner to buy it at a very favorable price and then turn around, knock down the current facility and build luxury condos.

Elizabeth listened intently as she took notes. "Go on. This is all very fascinating."

"When the center opened they decided to have someone mess up things a bit, scare the owners, and convince them to sell. That was supposed to be me. They wanted the owners to believe they had made a major mistake and find a way to walk away."

"And what happened?"

"They reneged on their offer on what they were going to pay me. They also changed their mind and wanted some very aggressive action against the people involved."

"Like what? What did they want you to do?"

"To the point of kidnapping and murder. I wanted none of that and walked away. That's when decided to have that second rate hood from Chicago, Vincent Check, become a resident, infiltrate the organization per se and cause trouble."

"So what happened to Check? Did Mike Long and friends have him killed?"

"Well this is where it gets even more complicated. The mob had their eyes on the property as well and accidentally found out that Vincent Check was working for the Long group. They didn't like that at all, and had him killed. There was also the matter of the missing gold. For years it had been rumored that ten million dollars in gold bars that had been taken in a heist from Fort Knox had made its way to California and wound up being hidden at the Alta Mira. Apparently the eccentric guy who built the Alta Mira had ties to the mob. Several years ago when some remodeling was being done at the Alta Mira a workman found a dozen gold bars buried in one of the walls. This caught everyone's attention, especially the mob that felt they owned this gold in the first place."

"Why are you telling me all this? What do you want out of this? And why have you waited so long to come forward?"

"I'm sick and tired of this group of people trying to control everything that goes on in Sausalito. What they're trying to do isn't right. I'm looking to turn state's witness and wind up in some kind of witness protection program. Can you help? I'm fearful for my life. I know they're coming after me."

"I can't guarantee a thing, but I think I can help. Let's get you in a safe place tonight."

Elizabeth made a reservation for Summers at a Travelodge on Lombard Street in San Francisco and promised to pick up the bill. "Let's put you there for a couple days. I'm going to get you in touch with my good friend, Stacey Gordon, from the Sausalito Police. We'll try to set that up for as early as tomorrow. Don't worry. I will come to that meeting with you."

He thanked her and seemed genuinely moved that Elizabeth was so interested in his safety. She knew she was responsible for the situation he now found himself in and had to assure he was safe from those wishing him harm. She was tempted to ask the San Francisco Police to keep an eye on him that evening but decided not to. She thought the fewer people who knew where he was the better.

She drove away hoping she had done the right thing and that Summers would still be alive in the morning. Summers had put a lot of trust in her, and she was taking that responsibility very seriously.

Thirty-Eight

Traffic was heavy, and my bus arrived in Tahoe City about 45 minutes late. I got off the bus, claimed my baggage and looked for a cab. Not seeing a cab anywhere in sight, I picked up the phone in the tiny bus terminal that was a direct line to Tahoe Taxi and asked them to come pick me up. Less than 15 minutes later the cab arrived. It was a yellow cab with "Tahoe Taxi" painted on its doors and trunk. My driver looked like someone who had been in Tahoe since the Summer of Love and no-one had told him the times had changed. He proudly wore his tie-died short, shorts, and Birkenstock sandals.

His license proudly displayed on the dashboard said his name was Fred Kowalski, I asked Fred to take me to the Tahoma Shores B&B. He grunted something that sounded like, "Sure" and pulled away towards the west shore of Lake Tahoe. About 15 minutes later we pulled up at the main building at Tahoma Shores. The fare was seven dollars even. I gave Fred a ten dollar bill and told him to keep the change. He helped me out with my bags and pulled away. I left my bags outside the door and walked up the stairs to the office. I knew I wouldn't be long.

"Ah, we've been expecting you," said a forgettable looking woman named Wanda sitting in the office. She pulled out a registration sheet and had me sign it. She also handed me a welcome letter from the owners. As I walked out the door she returned to her magazine, "Backyard Poultry."

"I want to remind you that I am her anonymously. If anyone comes by or calls, I am not here. No-one can know that I am here."

"We understand. We are putting you in the one cabin way in the back that doesn't have a name. That's about as low profile as we can get."

"Perfect." I climbed down the stairs, grabbed my luggage and walked towards the back of the property to my small cabin. It was painted in dark earth tones and was in dire need of a paint job. Inside was a king size bed, a small table with chairs and a TV. I put down my bags and lied down on my bed exhausted. The windows were open, and a cool breeze filled the room. I fell asleep and woke up two hours later.

The sun was just setting. I noticed an envelope on the table. My name was printed on the front. I thought it might be a welcome note from the owners. I walked over and opened the envelope. Inside was a written note that read, "Welcome to Tahoe, Scott. Raven."

My heart stopped. How did Raven know where I was? Did Raven follow me all the way up here from Sausalito? I ran to the office. It was closed. Did Wanda betray me and tell Raven where I was? I thought that unlikely. I briefly considered moving to another location around Tahoe but strangely felt safe for the moment. If Raven wanted me to be dead the opportunity was already there. He or she could have killed me while I slept. Raven was playing a game of cat and mouse with me. I had never owned a gun, but this was one time I wish I had owned one. I didn't feel like I was on a level playing field. However, I'm not sure I could use one and actually shoot someone.

I decided that I needed a car. It was late in the day. I called the 800 number for the major rental car companies and could not find any still open. I reserved a car with Avis for the following morning at a location at the small airport in South Lake Tahoe. I would take a cab there tomorrow morning; I shut and locked the windows. I pushed the table and chair up against the door. I knew that wouldn't help much but it made me feel better. This was the best I could do trying to protect myself.

Sleep didn't come easy that night. I briefly fell asleep and heard a commotion outside my door. The people in the cabin next to mine had a left a cooler with food out on their front porch and two bears were now breaking into it. I briefly turned my light back on and the shut it off and briefly went back to sleep. I woke up at 5AM, wide awake and frankly surprised I was still alive. I had slept in my clothes from the day before. I went to the bathroom and briefly freshened up. The Avis location opened at 7AM. I called for a taxi to pick me up a half hour prior. The B&B had my credit card imprint so I didn't have to worry about waiting around to pay them I would call later that morning to tell them I was gone. I simply wanted to disappear.

The taxi arrived 15 minutes after I called. I thought it might be Fred who brought me here from the bus station. It wasn't. It was an elderly man who proudly told me he had been driving a cab in Tahoe for 37 years. He was proud of that, and I wasn't going to take that away from him. I made meaningless small talk. He seemed pleased that I was interested in his career driving a cab in Tahoe. I suddenly knew more than I thought I would ever know about driving a taxi in Tahoe. It helped pass the time.

When I got in the cab I carefully looked to see if anyone was lurking in the shadows. I saw no-one. As we made our way to South Tahoe I was curious if anyone was following us. Once again I saw no-one. This puzzled me. I thought Raven would be hot in pursuit. Surely I would be able to find a safe place. Tahoe was so complex. There were all kinds of out of the way places one could disappear into and not be found. I had to drive around until I found the next place I would stay.

The man at the Avis counter asked what kind of car I was looking for. I told him I wanted something small and basic. I wanted to blend in with everyone else around the lake. The man wanted to know where I was staying. I told him I didn't know but would call him when I had found a place to spend the night. I probably should have just made up some bullshit location but decided to keep the high ground. He walked me out to a three year old blue Ford Focus. This was about as basic as one could get. He asked me if I needed a map. I told him that I probably knew the area better than he did. He didn't take kindly to my comment. I just smiled, grabbed my rental envelope, and drove off. After driving for ten minutes I pulled over to the side of the road and called the Embassy Suites in South Tahoe and reserved a room for two nights. I could always extend this reservation if need be. I just wanted to make sure I had a room secured for that night. I hoped it would be a safe place.

I pulled around the back of the Embassy Suites. I left my luggage in the car and went inside to check in. They had a suite available for me on the fifth floor, the top floor of the building. I had left the door open in my car. My bags were sitting in the back seat. I asked if someone could please bring my bags up.

Thirty-Nine

As promised Elizabeth Harris set up a meeting between Jeffrey Summers, Stacey
Gordon and the Special Agent Toland of the FBI. Everyone thought it best that this
Meeting is held in a neutral location. Elizabeth suggested they all meet in a conference
Room at the Chronicle that afternoon at 2.PM. Elizabeth reserved an out-of –the
way room on the third floor and let Summers know that she would personally pick
him up at 2:30 to safely bring him to the meeting. He promised to be waiting. Elizabeth
told him to bring his stuff. Chances are they wouldn't be coming back to the Travelodge.

Elizabeth briefed her editor on the entire Summers situation. They agreed they would
meet after that afternoon's meeting to discuss where they should go with the story. They
wanted to break this story before anyone else but also wanted to do so in a responsible
manner. They both hoped that the FBI would find a safe place for Summers to stay,
Elizabeth now felt responsible for Jeffrey Summers's well-being. They were opening up the
newspaper to all kinds of liability. She would have to be his advocate at the meeting with

Stacey Gordon and John Toland. She had to make sure Summers was taken care of.

She left the office at 2:15 and walked across the street to the garage where she had left her car, a two year old green Prius. She always parked on the basement level where it
was always easy to find a parking place as well as an easy to leave. When she got to the Travelodge on Lombard she found him waiting outside his room. She was outraged.

"What in the world are you doing outside?" she asked. "We don't want to make you anymore of a target than you already are. Gheez, I told you to wait in your room."

He apologized and got in the car. He seemed upset and didn't want to talk.

"Relax the best you can, Jeffrey," she said. "This should be a very good productive meeting. Things will be okay. I promise. We're not going to let anyone hurt you."

"I hope it wasn't a mistake calling you," he replied. "I normally have a very poorly developed sense of fear, but this terrifies me. I know the first chance they get they will try to
kill me."

"You're doing the right thing, Jeffrey. This is a very brave thing you are doing. It
says a lot about you and what you're all about. I know that it takes a lot of courage."

Rather than parking in the lot, Elizabeth found a meter in front of the building. This Sounded like a safer thing to do. She frankly could care less about getting a parking ticket. She parked, came around and opened the door for Jeffrey, and they entered the front door of the Chronicle Building. She led Jeffrey through security, and they caught a waiting elevator and went up to the fifth floor. She brought him to the conference room and asked if he had lunch.

"I'm not really hungry," he said, "but a cup of black coffee would really look good."

She left the room and returned minutes later with coffee in a silver Chronicle mug.

Stacey Gordon was the first to arrive. She was wearing civilian clothes. She felt that would be less intimidating than had she come in uniform. They made small talk about Sausalito and agreed it would be better to wait until Special Agent Toland arrived. He arrived 20 minutes later and apologized for his tardiness. Elizabeth offered Stacey Gordon and Special Agent Toland coffee. Both declined. Summers said he'd take a refill.

Elizabeth decided to kick-off the meeting. "I want to thank everyone for coming. I know you're all very busy. As know Jeffrey Summers approached me several weeks ago
with information regarding the scandal in Sausalito. We ran a couple short pieces, not having much more to go on and have thus stirred up a hornet's nest. I know your investigations have continued. Jeffrey approached me a couple days ago, wanting to go

public with me with who he was and to tell his story. He is afraid for his life, and I that I set up this meeting. Let's let Jeffrey talk and see what we can do to help him."

Stacey Gordon and Toland both shook their heads in agreement. They were anxious to get on with the meeting.

Stacey spoke. "Thanks for your cooperation, Mr. Summers. My name is Stacey Gordon
and I'm with the Sausalito Police Department. I've been the point person on this
investigation ever since Vincent Check was found dead in the Downtown park in our
city. Needless to say, I am most anxious to hear what you have to say. We're having a difficult time connecting the dots. There are many things that need clarification."

Toland jumped in. "Mr. Summers, I'm Special Agent John Toland of the San Francisco office of the Federal Bureau of Investigation. We became interested in this case because
of Vincent Check, a small-time hood who's been on our radar screen for some time. He was a member of the Chicago mob. We're still not sure how or why he wound up in San Francisco. I too can't wait to hear your story."

Summers took everyone through the complete story starting off when he was originally approached by Mayor Mike Long to do a "special project." He had no fear and was willing to do anything for money."

"He basically wanted me to make life hell for the Alta Mira's owners. He wanted to terrify them so they would sell. He didn't care what I would have to do in order to accomplish this end result. He suggested I kidnap some of the key people and if needed kill them. I'm sure you'll run my record and see that I've done some things that I'm not proud of but have never done anything of that ilk. I am not into violence."

"We've already done that, Mr. Summers," said Toland. "I agree you have never done anything that extreme."

"The end result was supposed to be the owners of the Alta Mira would give up and sell the property at a deeply discounted rate. Mike Long assembled his group of investors, that's the group you found in Check's pocket. They were ready to move on a dime. They were certain that once the Alta Mira was indeed up for sale they would prevail in the fire sale."

"So how did Vincent Check fit into the equation?" asked Stacey.

"When I backed out, needless to say, they were outraged. They needed to find someone quickly to stir the pot. Mike Long had some connections with the mob and happened to stumble across Vincent Check. They decided to up the ante and have him move into the Alta Mira as a resident. That way he would have direct access to everything and anything."

"There's got to be something more to it than that," said Toland.

"There is." Summers went on to explain the story of the missing shipment of gold that's supposedly hidden in the darkness of Alta Mira.. Stacey and Toland were fascinated.

"Wow at over forty grand a month that was an expensive move," said Stacey.

"These guys are rolling in dough. They thought it would be a good investment," replied Summers.

"So why was Check whacked?" asked Toland. "Why did they want him dead?"

"The mob really wanted the Alta Mira for the reasons I just explained. They found he was working with Long and his cohorts. They were really pissed and decided to send message to Long. It's as simple as that. Believe me the Alta Mira was worth a lot of dough. Both Long's group and the mob figured they could have put over 40 condos on that land.

They realistically thought with the right zoning and master plan they could realize over a hundred million from this land. This is probably the most coveted real estate in Marin County. People have been trying to figure out for years how to get their hands on it. Add all that onto finding the missing gold and you've really got something."

Elizabeth jumped in. "Jeffrey is fearful for his life. He is way too high profile and Knows his life is in danger. What can you do to help him?"

"Are you willing to turn government witness and testify in court?" asked Toland.

"I am on the condition you protect me." There are people out there who would like to kill me. I'm surprised they haven't by now."

Toland continued. "Give me the key to your place. We'll send someone over there to get some of your stuff. I can have you in a safe house tonight. We'll be very careful that no one sees us coming or going. We do this all the time." Stacey rolled her eyebrows.

"Wow, this is moving quickly," said Summers.

"Are you in or are you out?" asked Toland

"I have no choice. Of course I'm in."

They talked for an additional three hours. Stacey and Toland agreed that their superiors should talk to determine jurisdiction which they agreed would probably fall into the hands of the FBI. Summers seemed relieved to have told his story. He was grateful for the promised help and was still doubtful whether or not they could truly keep him safe. He was terrified of being killed.

Elizabeth agreed that the Chronicle would sit on the story for a very limited Amount of time, but the desire was to break the story before the competition, and the competition was fierce, especially coming from the television stations. In a time when the Chronicle was hurting and losing circulation, a story like this would sell papers and further advance Elizabeth's position at the paper. However, the story had to be done right the first time. Although she wanted to believe everything Jeffrey Summers was saying, she wasn't completely sure if she could. She certainly could understand why someone would want to step forward and do the right thing, but why did he wait so long? She had made the leap of faith in believing Summers and introducing him to the authorities. She hoped she had done the right thing. Her credibility was also at stake. This was a very delicate story and had to be handled carefully.

She picked up the phone and called several people she knew and trusted in Sausalito. The feedback was pretty much the same from everyone she spoke with. Jeffrey Summers was
indeed someone who always pushed the envelope, but at the end of the day he was a straight-shooter and told the truth. There were just too many warning flags for her to be completely comfortable. In her niche of journalism there was no margin of error. One inaccurate story could ruin a promising career. There were also powerful forces out there who would like to kill her Sausalito stories.

Forty

I slept later than I had planned. I looked at the digital clock on the nightstand in my bedroom in the Embassy Suites. It was almost 8:30 AM. I rolled out of bed and into the
Shower. The free breakfast down in the lobby ended at nine, and I wanted to take advantage of it. I made it with 10 minutes to spare and helped myself to some barely warm scrambled eggs, bacon, toast, and juice. As was my .custom I carefully lo I walked around to see if anyone might remotely resemble an assassin. I knew this was a silly habit and to keep reminding myself that Raven could be almost anyone. There was a definite ebb and flow to my paranoia. I knew damn well Raven could be almost anyone.

I decided to lay low today and carefully think through my situation and evaluate the alternatives. I was running for my life. I hadn't spoken with Julie since I arrived in Tahoe and
decided to give her a call. She sounded funny when I called. Something was wrong, but I couldn't quite put my finger on it.

So how's the weather in San Diego?" she asked. "Have you been to the beach?"

"Bright and sunny," I replied. I really didn't know but thought this was a safe answer since it's almost always perfect weather in San Diego.

"Scott. I'm looking at San Diego weather on the Internet. It's raining. You're not in San Diego are you?"

"No I'm not."

"Why did you lie to me? Are you with another woman?" I could hear the hurt in her voice. "I thought we were always completely honest with each other."

"What do you mean, 'Of course not?' You're not where you told me you were going. Just where are you, Scott?"

"I can't tell you? Bear with me just a little bit longer."

"Why not? What are you hiding from me? Where are you, Scott?"

"I just can't tell you quite yet? Bear with me just a little bit long

"What does that mean?" She started. Click. She hung up on me. I couldn't blame her. Now my wife, my best friend, was upset with me. I wanted to tell her what was going on but couldn't. I couldn't get her involved in this ugly mess. I decided to let her cool off and call her back the following day. It will be hard to wait that long, but typically when she's so upset with me a day is all it usually took for her to come around. She didn't have it in her DNA to stay mad long.

Against my better judgment I decided to go for a run. I asked the front desk if they had any suggestions as to where to go for my run. The young woman behind the counter gave me a map with three different routes. I chose the longest route. I needed something to help burn off my stress which was now running rampant. My run was just less than five miles. I returned feeling better but still feeling bad that I had left Julie so upset. I felt helpless. I didn't know what to do. When Julie was hurting I was hurting.

When I got back to the hotel I found a chair by the pool and sat down to relax. I took out my Blackberry hoping that there might have been a message waiting from Julie. There was not. I briefly debated whether or not to call Julie. I decided not to. This would accomplish nothing and make both of us feel even worse. I closed my eyes for a moment and fell asleep which was not what I wanted to do. This left me vulnerable to anything Raven might have wanted to do to me. I woke up about an hour later and rode the elevator up to my room and jumped in the shower. The hot water felt good beating against my body. I climbed out of the shower, put on a fresh pair of jeans and a black golf shirt. I noticed the message light on the phone blinking. I called the front desk. It took them several minutes to retrieve the message. I had no idea who might have known I was there.

"Yes sir, Mr. Butler. You have one message. It says 'Hi, Scott. See you soon. Raven.'"

Forty-One

I felt Raven closing in on me. Raven knew where I was. Why didn't Raven try to try already to take my life? Raven was playing with me. This was some kind of weird sadistic game. This was truly the cat playing with the mouse. I decided to jump in my car and just drive not knowing what my ultimate destination might be. I refused to just wait around for Raven to find me and fulfill the contract.

I used the check-out feature on my room TV and quietly slipped out the back door. I threw my bags in the trunk of my car and headed back up the west shore of Lake Tahoe. I was looking for someplace, any place to hide. About a half hour up the road was the old Kaiser mansion, Fleur du Lac. This is where several key scenes of "The Godfather" were filmed. Much of the grounds have been converted to luxury condos. I was surprised to find the security gate was open. I drove on the grounds looking for some place that I might be able to stay. Unfortunately there was no hotel on the expansive grounds. I was even looking for a vacant condo that I might have been able to break into and hide. I didn't believe there was but had to try.

I headed further up the coast. It was lunch time. Although I wasn't very hungry I decided to stop. One of my favorite restaurants was ahead. It's the Sunnyside Inn, the iconic California cuisine restaurant. I asked for a table on the deck overlooking the parking lot and main entrance. That way I could keep me eyes on any suspicious individuals who might be entering the restaurant. I was almost surprised that Raven didn't pull up right after me, come in the restaurant, and finish me off. But I was developing a definite appreciation for Raven and knew he or she was smarter than that. I wondered how Raven had gotten into this line of work.

I ordered the garlic fries and a bottle of Beck's. My food came out of the kitchen quickly. I had just finished my first bottle of Beck's and ordered another. I wondered why I wasn't drinking my Grey Goose martinis, but beer sounded like a better bet in this restaurant. The fries were excellent, although I didn't eat them all. I had other things on my mind and wasn't that hungry. For no apparent reason I felt safe in the restaurant. Raven surely knew what kind of car I was driving and could have easily found me. I ordered a third beer and left the restaurant three hours after I got there. I was tempted to stay a bit longer but knew if I had any more to drink my driving would be impaired. This was not the time to get stopped for a DUI. Or maybe it was.

Needing a place to spend the night I pondered the possibilities. I remember a wonderful B&B that Julie and I had stayed at a few years ago. It's called the Chaney House and was on West Lake Boulevard about a mile from the restaurant. I didn't bother to call and drove right over to the Chaney House. It was a marvelous old building, resembling a castle, built in the mid-1920s by an Italian stone mason. I entered the building and found the office near the end of the hall when you walked in the door. I was glad to hear that they had one last room available. I asked them to not tell anyone who might ask if I was there. They too politely nodded as if they had heard this request before. They gave me my key and directed me to my room. I told them I had no idea how long I would be staying. That said that was just fine and to please give them regular updates.

I had forgotten how impressive the building was on the inside. It was obvious that the Chaney family took great pride in their little treasure. The building had 18 inch stone walls, gothic arches, and a massive floor to ceiling fireplace in the common area. My room was on the second floor near the back of the building. It was small but very quaint. It had a four poster bed with an antique quilt covering it; there was a couch on one wall and a small flat screen that seemed strangely out of place sitting on the dresser. I double-locked the door and sat down on the couch. I grabbed my phone and for a brief moment was tempted to call Julie but decided not to. As much as I wanted to talk to her, what would I say? "I miss you. I love you. But I can't tell you where I AM." I decided a phone call would be very painful for both of us and put my phone away. I sat on the couch for the next couple hours, my life flashing before my eyes. Things don't normally scare me, but I was frozen in fear.

I weighed my alternatives. I could continue to run. This meant that I risked never seeing Julie again. That was something I could not even consider doing. The only decent alternative appeared to throwing me at the mercy of the justice system, let them know what I know about the mob murder for hire situation that I had been involved with and throw myself at the mercy of the system. I wanted protection for myself and Julie.

At first I wasn't sure who I should be talking to. The Sausalito Police were not the answer. Should I contact the local authorities up here in Tahoe? That too was not the answer. The FBI was the place I had to go. I went on the Internet from my Blackberry looking for the number of the FBI in Sacramento and was pleasantly surprised to see that they had a small resident office in South Tahoe. I dialed the number and got the office's voice mail. I left my name and number and got a call back a half hour later. Special Agent Rita Glastris returned my call. I explained to her that I had information regarding a crime and wanted to meet.

"Would you like to come in today?" she asked. She sounded worried that I might change my mind. "I will wait for you as long as you need me to."

Although I just wanted to get this over with I asked if tomorrow morning would work. I needed the night to pull myself together and practice my story. I wanted to make sure I had my key messages down pat.

"How about 11 in the morning?" she asked. "Do you need directions?"

"That's okay I'll find you."

"Don't expect much when you get here. It's just me and a secretary, and I'm losing her at the end of the month because a budget cutback. Call if you get lost. It's really not too difficult to find. Are you sure you don't want to come by today?"

I hung up, relieved that my nightmare might be at long last coming to an end. I hoped Special Agent Glastris would help me. I had no idea where my visit would lead me. They could very well just arrest me for the role I played in arranging three deaths. There was nothing else I could do. I had to take the chance. She sounded like she wanted to help. I couldn't ask for any more than that. It was time for some closure.

I checked the locks on the door and window and lay down to take a quick nap before going out for some dinner. I was awakened an hour by a tweet on my Blackberry indicating that someone had left me a text. I was hoping it might be Julie. I clicked on the text icon and a message popped up. "Scott. It looks like the Chaney House is a lovely place to stay. Too bad you won't be there much longer. Raven."

Forty-Two

Jeffrey Summers woke up Thursday morning in the safe house he had been living in ever since his first meeting with Stacey Gordon and Special Agent John Toland. The house was under constant surveillance by armed FBI agents and San Francisco Police. Although he was grateful for the protection he never felt completely safe. He was the only resident of the house and was going crazy being by himself. From time to time someone would come in with food. He would try to engage them in small talk just to have someone to talk to. He wasn't sure how long he would be there and wondered whether or not they might take him somewhere else. The place was comfortable enough. He had a fully stocked refrigerator, cable TV, and most of the comforts of home. The only thing negative was the fact it was so damn small. If he was claustrophobic he would have been in serious trouble. It was a small nondescript house built in the 1950s. He wondered who else might have stayed there under protective custody. He would ask but never got an answer. He didn't need to know.

The prior day the complete story had broke in the Chronicle. Summers was proud of the job Elizabeth Harris had done in piecing it together. The story broke to coincide with the arrests the night before of Mike Long and everyone else whose name appeared on the now infamous list that was found on Vincent Check's body. The FBI, joined by the Sausalito Police had swept down on the town at 11 .PM the prior evening and rounded up the suspects. They were being held in the Federal lock-up in the old Federal Building in Downtown San

Francisco. Attorneys representing the suspects were voicing righteous indignation to the media. "How could these pillars of society be suspected of something so sinister?"

"Easy,' commented Spencer Adams, US Attorney for the Northern District of California. "It all had to do with greed. We are dealing with dangerous individuals. There is a governmental crime spree going on in Sausalito. This is something we must squash right now. We can't let things go any further. Trusted elected government officials are acting very badly."

That morning Mike Long and the others suspects appeared before US Magistrate Lewis Sullivan for a bail hearing. The courtroom was flooded with press and other interested parties. Although the federal government asked for remand, Magistrate Sullivan set bail at $1,000.000 for each individual. Many people were outraged and thought this wasn't enough. Within three hours bail bondmen had been summoned and everyone had been released. All of the defendants had the financial resources to secure $100,000, ten percent of the bond Amount necessary to be released.

Against the advice of his attorney, Mike Long called a news conference that afternoon at Paradise Bay restaurant in Sausalito. He originally wanted to have it at City Hall, but city Manager Sam Holman denied the request. "You're on your own," he told Long. "The city is embarrassed enough as it is. We can't be conducting a potentially volatile press conference on city property. You've opened us up to enough viability as it is. If I would allow you to do your little show on city property they should run me out of town.'

The press conference was well-attended and a disaster for the defendants. Satellite trucks filled up valuable parking places in the parking lot. Mike Long made opening comments blasting everyone from the media to the FBI to the Sausalito Police. The other suspects in attendance groaned. Things got especially contentious when questioning started. Terry Quinn from KGO-TV threw the first salvo. "Mr. Mayor, Vincent Check was a known member of the Chicago mob. He was found dead in the park right here in Sausalito. Inside his coat pocket was a piece of paper with the names and phone numbers of yourself and your fellow defendants. Can you please explain that?"

Long knew he would get that question, but not as the first thing coming out of a reporter's mouth. If he had developed talking points prior to the press conference he had forgotten them. He babbled for awhile piecing several incoherent sentences together and finally said, "I have no idea." There was silence. The assembled media was shocked.

Jim Squires, another defendant leaned over and asked Long if he could take over answering questions. Squires was far more articulate than Long and wanted to defuse the situation before it got any worse. Long was insulted and told him to "Fuck off" which was picked up loud and clear by the broadcast outlets. He had fired the first salvo, and the media were ready to pounce on him and answer.

The next two reporters, Jerry Harrison from CBS5 and Tom Mason from KRON-TV followed the same line of questioning. Finally an exasperated Mike Long who had all that he could take declared the press conference over, and made a dash for his car in the parking lot, leaving Sid Emmett behind whom he had driven to Paradise Bay. Emmett came running after him yelling, "What the fuck, Mike!" Long kept driving away. He never looked back.

Inside Jim Squires volunteered to answer other questions but most of the press had already left. They wanted to interview the mayor, and he conveniently left. The other suspects dreaded watching the news that evening. Mike Long made them all look very guilty. Squires followed several members of the media into the parking lot but they were not interested in speaking with him Mike Long had made a fool of himself, and they had their story. Nothing that Jim Squires could possibly say would interest them.

It was true that some of the suspects were more involved with the scheme than others, but in the eyes of the law they were all guilty. It's true that you're innocent until proven guilty, but the court of public opinion it's really guilty until proven innocent. In three weeks the defendants would once again appear in Federal Court to enter a plea. Mike Long had made a serious strategic error by having the press conference in the first place. The defendants and their attorneys would do the best they can to recover. He was a loose cannon and was hurting their case. Somehow he thought that being Mayor of tiny little Sausalito made him above the law. He would soon learn this wasn't the case.

The next day the defendants, led by Mike Long, filed suit against the San Francisco Chronicle for printing the story. Elizabeth was delighted. This added credibility to her story. She was already preparing a follow up story that would run in two days. The story would go into the scandal in greater detail with valuable information from Stacey Gordon, who would continue to be identified as "An anonymous source intimately connected with the investigation."

A second suit was filed asking that the Chronicle reveal its sources for the stories. This suit was quickly thrown out by the presiding judge in San Francisco Superior Court who wasn't about to pierce the curtain of confidentiality between the media and its confidential sources. This was one of those nuisance suits that everyone knew would be filed but would get nowhere. Mike Long was outraged when the judge handed down his decision but followed the demands of others and didn't go after the judge through the press. He would choose the right moment to accuse the government of persecution.

In the meantime Jeffrey Summers would sit and wait. Patience was never his greatest virtue, and he was being tested beyond belief. He knew he would be there for the long run or perhaps shipped out of state until the trials would begin. He didn't care. All he wanted to be was safe. His one salvation was that the house had a full cable package, and he could watch whatever he wanted whenever he wanted. He was getting a little tired of the food, and those guarding him said they would see what they could do but so far no luck.

He wanted to reach out to his friends and family and let them know he was alright. But they knew he was the ultimate survivor and would wind up just fine. However, Summers wasn't all that sure himself. He had a hard time sleeping and very little interest in food. He kept creating scenarios in his mind how those who wished him harm would penetrate the tight security at the safe house and kill him. It worried him whenever a new person assigned to protect him would show up. He would wonder whether that person was who he claimed to be or someone who was coming to kill him.

He briefly contemplated taking off and running. It soon hit home that he would be far safer in a situation like this where he was being protected.

Forty-Three

I was now convinced that Raven was camped outside this building knowing that I would have to come out sooner or later and would kill me at that time. I had my date with the FBI tomorrow morning and had to find a way to stay alive till then. My first thought was to call the FBI and have them come and get me now. It was late. I called and got a recording. I wasn't confident that anyone would get back to me and didn't leave a message. I briefly entertained the idea of calling the local Police but couldn't be sure who would actually show up was the local authorities rather than Raven. I also knew that sooner or later Raven would lose his or her patience and come storming in here to get me.

I came up with an idea that I hoped would work. I would fake sever chest pains and have the B&B call an ambulance and take me to the hospital. Surely Raven would not be able to penetrate a group of firefighters and cops. I had forgotten my high blood pressure medication at home. I was highly dependent on that to control my blood pressure and already starting to feel ill. Add that on top of the stress I'm under right now I'm sure it would be sky high. I reached for the phone and begun what would have to be an Academy Award performance. I had to be convincing.

"Hello," I gasped. "This is Scott Butler. "I checked in this afternoon. I am having horrible chest pains and think I'm having a heart attack. Please call an Ambulance."

Within moments the wife of the owner appeared at my door. "You poor dear," she said. "My husband is calling the rescue squad right now. You'll be ok. I will stay with you until they come. I will pray for you until they arrive." She was so sweet and caring that I almost felt bad this was an elaborate hoax.

I was rolling on the bed, moaning, and grasping my chest. Minutes later the Douglas County Rescue Squad arrived in full force. I was very impressed. Manning the ambulance was two men and a young woman. They took my vitals and phoned them into Barton Hospital in South Tahoe where they would be taking me. Sure enough my blood pressure was off the charts. They put me on the gurney and carried me down to the ambulance.

Waiting outside was a police car that would give us an escort to the hospital. I signaled for the police officer that I wanted to talk to him. When he came over to me I whispered in his ear, "I'm due to meet with the FBI in the morning. I am fearful for my life. Please don't let anything happen to me." We headed down West Shore Highway lights flashing and sirens blaring. I wondered what Raven thought of this spectacle. This point was mine, advantage Scott. My adrenalin was going through the roof. For some strange reason I was starting to enjoy the cat and mouse game. I wondered where Raven was right now.

We arrived at the hospital 15 minutes later. A team of doctors and nurses met us at the ER. I was taken off the ambulance and wheeled into the ER. Once again they took my vitals my blood pressure was worse than it had been when they came to get me. My pulse was also elevated. They wheeled over an EKG machine, hooked me up and moments later I heard a doctor say, "The EKG results were inconclusive." That's exactly what I wanted to hear. They hooked me up to an IV and started feeding me various meds. Another doctor, a distinguished looking man in his 60s came over and said, "Mr. Butler, we're not sure what's going on with you, but we're going to keep you overnight to make sure nothing serious is going on with you. If everything goes well tonight we'll discharge you in the morning. My guess is that you will be just fine." This was good news. I would safely spend the night in the hospital and meet with Special Agent Rita Glastris of the FBI in the morning. It looked like I had outsmarted Raven.

A burly African-American nurse named Angel wheeled me up to my room I asked him how secure the hospital was. He gave me a funny look wondering why this was a concern of mine.

"This is an incredibly secure place," he chuckled. "They're putting you up in the ICU. Nobody is allowed up there that doesn't belong. And then at 8.PM the hospital goes on complete lockdown. There is security at every entrance. No worries. You'll be safe. None the less, I've got your back, Scott. You can take that to the bank." I told the nurse I wanted to make one phone call. He told me he wasn't supposed to let me do that but handed me my cell phone and told me to "make it quick." I called the South Tahoe FBI office and left a message for Special Agent Glastris that I had just been admitted to Barton Hospital with chest pains, was still fearful for my life, and was fully expecting to be at our meeting in the morning. Angel smiled with an all-knowing nod.

I was grateful he didn't ask me to explain why I was so concerned. He gave me a knowing smile figuring that something was going on and that it was none of his business. I felt that I finally was one step ahead of Raven. I was confident I was in a safe place.

When I got to my room a male nurse came in and introduced himself as Randy. He said that he would be going off duty in a couple hours and wasn't sure who would be taking care of me that night. They had a few people call in sick. He said they might have to pull someone off another floor so that ICU was fully staffed. "We can always find someone to fill in," he said. "Don't worry. You will be well cared for."

"I don't know about you," he said. "I think some people know they have sick days coming and find any excuse to use them. I would rather be at work."

I told him I knew what he meant. He hooked up a new IV and carefully pushed the syringe of meds into the IV drip. I intently watched and wondered how long it took him to learn how to do that.

"This is good stuff," he said. "You'll be feeling mighty fine in just a few minutes. He was right. I fell asleep almost immediately waking up 90 minutes later. Randy was bringing me my food. It was turkey and some kind of rice. As bad as it looked I was hungry. If nothing else I could always just eat the Jell-O.

"Unfortunately this isn't haute cuisine," he said. "They keep things pretty bland in the ICU. It is what it is. Anyway, if I don't see you, have a good evening. I'll see you in the morning. I'm sure whomever is here will take very good care of you."

I thanked him for his kindness and downed my turkey and mystery rice. The cherry Jell-O was the highlight of my meal. Also on my trail was a small container of apple juice which I quickly drank as well. A nurse's aide came by a little later to pick up my tray. She asked how I was feeling. I said a lot better. I sat there and thought about Julie and the hell she must be going through right now. There was absolutely nothing I could do about it. I felt helpless. I'm sure by now she called Roy Wiegand. He undoubtedly covered for me the best he could but by now she knows I'm not with him. What must she think? AM I off on a fling with another woman? By now I would hope she would know that's not the truth. If everything goes well with the FBI tomorrow I will call her, come clean, and beg her forgiveness. I have been blessed with so many good things in life and its all come down to laying in a hospital bed praying for my salvation. I had to make it through this ordeal. There's got to be a happy ending. Julie and I have had too good of a life together to let it end because of this incident.

It has been years since I prayed let alone gone to church. If I wasn't hooked up to my IV I would have gotten down on my knees to pray. I prayed the Our Father, Glory Be, and the Hail Mary. I knew I would remember something from all those years of Catholic School. I even considered praying, "Jesus lay me down to sleep."

I looked at the clock on the wall outside the window of my room. It was 9:40 in the evening. I was tired but a bit too wired to get to sleep. I was eagerly anticipating my meeting the following morning with the FBI. I went over in my mind everything I wanted to tell them. It was a complicated story, and I didn't want to leave anything out.

There was a knock on the door. It was a nurse with short dark hair in light green scrubs. She was in her mid- 30s and had a very gentle way about her. You could tell that she probably had been the star of her class in nursing school. She slowly approached my bed.

"I'm here to give you something to help you sleep," she softly said.

She injected the contents of the syringe into my IV drip. Almost immediately I could feel its effect. I became very sleepy and had a hard time keeping my eyes open. The thought of getting some sleep sounded great. I felt safe. I knew that when I got up I could call Julie and explain everything. Things would be just fine. She would understand.

"So I guess you'll be taking care of me tonight," I said. "What's your name?"

"Scott, you can call me Raven."

Epilogue

The long arm of justice typically moves slowly and deliberately. The United States Attorney for the Northern District of California, Spencer Adams, made every attempt to negotiate a plea bargain with Mike Long and the other defendants in the Sausalito Alta Mira case. He ran into a stone wall. Mike Long was showing both arrogance and stupidity by refusing a plea bargain. With Jeffrey Summers's testimony they had a powerful case against Long. The others initially fell into lockstep with Long and refused to negotiate. Then cooler heads prevailed. Jim Squires convinced everyone to turn government evidence against Long in exchange for immunity. Sid Emmett was the first to agree which surprised Squires. By this time the government knew Mike Long was the mastermind of the scheme, and thus he was the only one they truly had any interest in prosecuting.

Even with the others turning against Long he refused any kind of plea bargain. He was convinced he was above the law and somehow would be vindicated. In the process he went through three different attorneys, the first two quit from pure frustration, the third he fired. Each time he hired new counsel it delayed the start of Long's trial. Judge Edwin Jackson warned Long to be careful with his selection of his fourth attorney and wouldn't allow any further changes of counsel. The pending trial received very generous media coverage and the entire Bay Area legal community realized Mike Long was the client from hell. Long had a difficult getting Bay Area representation and wound up hiring a Los Angeles based attorney to represent him. The calendar of the District Court in San Francisco was very full, and

Mike Long's trial was to begin in six months. That would also give his new attorney plenty of time to get up to speed while encouraging Long to keep his mouth shut. The government had an open and shut case against Long, and everyone wondered what in the world Long's counsel could put on as a defense. Long's new counsel strongly advised him to accept a generous plea bargain but he wouldn't budge. Court insiders speculated that this attorney would beg the judge to let him off the case.

In the meantime Jeffrey Summers was officially brought into the Federal Witness Protection Program. With a completely new identity he was whisked out of San Francisco for a small town in Colorado where he would remain until called to testify in Mike Long's trial. In all likelihood he would be moved to another safe location with a completely new identity after the trial. He was having a hard time leaving Northern California but knew this sacrifice would have to be made in order to assure his safety. He started over before and knew he could do it again. He was curious what his name would be. It was hard to acknowledge that he would never see his family and friends again. For once in his life he had done a good and admirable deed. No-one would ever be able to take that away from him.

Elizabeth Harris hit a home run with her Sausalito series of stories. They became very popular and received considerable reader comment. News stand circulation for the Chronicle was up considerably, People followed every development of the shady deals in Sausalito. In addition to her on-going series on Sausalito Elizabeth would also be covering Mike Long's trial and everything leading up to it. She had found the career-defining story that she had been dreaming of. She knew she was up for the challenge. She started searching for her next big story and still checked her hotline several times every day.

Sam Holman, City Manager of Sausalito handled damage control as well as he could, Mike Long was immediately removed as Mayor and the entire council was gone as well. A special election was scheduled for two months out. The list of people running for city council seats was long and contained the names of citizens with stellar reputations. The city would find itself in very good hands and continue to prosper. The scandal proved to be a blip in the long proud history of Sausalito that dated back to the colorful1850s. People frequently forget that at one time the Mayor of Sausalito was a former madam, Sally Stanford. Nothing that ever happens in Sausalito tends to surprise many people.

Stacey Gordon received considerable praise for her work on the case and was given additional responsibility with the Sausalito Police Department. She remained the "anonymous source." in all Chronicle stories. She and Elizabeth Harris became fast friends. She was encouraged to take the sergeant's test the next time it was given. She started dating a great guy that Elizabeth introduced her to. She won the support and respect of her superiors and fellow officers that she had been seeking since joining the force.

The owners of the Alta Mira decided to keep the rehab center open in spite of everything that had happened. It was very difficult weathering the storm, and they had gotten through it just fine. The ill feelings of residents of Sausalito had waned considerably and the Alta Mira was largely accepted. New things would come up to divert the thoughts of the good people of Sausalito to other areas of controversy. The city dropped its suit against the Alta Mira. In a recent renovation an additional untold amount of gold was found leading speculation to the fact that the missing 12 million dollars in gold is still hidden in the darkest reaches of the Alta Mira.

Julie Butler found out she was pregnant. Everyone in her life was thrilled. The male hand on her belly felt the baby's first kick. Some things were just meant to be.

About the Author

Terrence Brejla is a proud native of Chicago and currently lives in the San Francisco Bay Are. This is his fourth novel and sixth book. He is a high profile editor and very much in demand. As a writer his influences include Raymond Chandler and Ross MacDonald. He is a graduate of Drake University and remains hopeful that his beloved Chicago White Sox will repeat 2005 and win another World Series

www.ingramcontent.com/pod-product-compliance
Lightning Source LLC
Chambersburg PA
CBHW072232170626
46813CB00003B/1189